THE MEDICINE-MAN

W. C. Tuttle

Life sure is dealing Bud Daley a mean hand. His entire stock of Triangle-D cattle is stolen, Sheriff Breed won't help him because of a personal grudge, his wife May is being propositioned by a disloyal money-lender, and Bud's friends, Uncle Jimmy and the huge Sody, are short on ideas and long on arguments. And when Bud is arrested for murder and the robbery of the Modoc bank, Hashknife Hartley and Sleepy Stevens are determined to help reunite May with her persecuted husband.

THE MEDICINE-MAN
A Hashknife Story

W. C. Tuttle

Curley Publishing, Inc.
South Yarmouth, Ma.

Library of Congress Cataloging-in-Publication Data

Tuttle, W. C. (Wilbur C.), 1883–
  Medicine man / W. C. Tuttle.
    p. cm.
  1. Large type books. I. Title.
  [PS3539.U988M44 1990]
  813′.52—dc20
  ISBN 0–7927–0382–0 (lg. print)   89–48473
  ISBN 0–7927–0383–9 (pbk.: lg. print)   CIP

Published in Large Print by arrangement with Donald MacCampbell, Inc. in the United States, Canada, the U.K. and British Commonwealth.

Distributed in Great Britain, Ireland and the Commonwealth by CHIVERS LIBRARY SERVICES LIMITED, Bath BA1 3HB, England.

Printed in Great Britain

THE MEDICINE-MAN

CHAPTER I

Bud Daley sat humped over his wash-bench near the kitchen door of his unpretentious little ranch-house, staring with moody blue eyes across the hills. The wash-bench was sloppy with soapsuds, plain evidence that Bud had performed his ablutions in a violent manner.

And as he sat looking moodily into space, he dangled a none-too-clean towel in his hands. Just behind him, leaning against the side of the kitchen door, stood Mrs. Daley, a thoughtful frown on her pretty face. She was dressed in a plain calico dress, faded from many washings; a girlish looking woman whose crown of glorious auburn hair tumbled in unruly fashion about her face.

Bud's visible attire consisted of a battered sombrero, a thin blue shirt, wide open at the neck, a pair of bat-winged chaps, boots, and holstered gun. His thin face was decorated with several days' growth of beard. Down in the little corral, which was hooked to the long, low barn, a roan horse, sweat-marked, rolled wearily.

Bud's eyes turned from the panorama of

1

low hills, which swept away across the Modoc ranges, and his fingers searched his pockets for tobacco and cigarette papers.

"Bud, are you sure?" Mrs. Daley spoke softly, a trifle hopefully.

"Yeah," Bud nodded and licked the edge of the paper, "I reckon it's a fact, May."

"Then it means that we're – broke?"

"Broke?"

The match burned Bud's fingers, and he snapped it away as he turned and looked at her.

"May, we're worse than that. I still owe Cleve Lavelle five thousand dollars."

"As much as that, Bud?"

There were tears in her voice. Bud laughed shortly and got to his feet.

"Just that much, May."

"But – but where have the cattle gone? Surely –"

"They've been stolen!" said Bud savagely. "Somebody has rustled every head of Triangle-D stock in the Modoc country. By gosh, we haven't even got a hide nor a horn to show.

"I told Cleve Lavelle. He was at the round-up, May. They were all there; every puncher in this country. I tell you, we combed every inch of the county, and there wasn't a cattleman there, except me, that wasn't satisfied."

"Was Uncle Jimmy Miller there, Bud?"

"Yeah, he was there. He exploded over it. Just the same as told me I was a damn liar. But he found out that I was right. Oh, we're broke; that's a cinch."

Bud threw the towel aside and backed against the wall.

"But, Bud, we must have had close to five hundred head," said Mrs. Daley. "Why, you can't lose five hundred head of cattle."

"Can't we?" Bud laughed bitterly. "I wish you was right, May. I kept sayin' the same thing – until I had it proved to me. Somebody just – well –" Bud shrugged his shoulders wearily – "they took 'em, thasall."

"Well –" Mrs. Daley sighed deeply and patted him on the shoulder – "we're not very lucky, Bud. Dinner is ready."

"I'm not hungry, May. It kinda hits me in the pit of m' stummick."

"Starving won't help you any, dear."

"I s'pose not." Bud grinned and shook his head. "I reckon I've got to keep m' head up and m' stummick full. I wish –"

Two riders swung around the corner of the cottonwood clump beyond the barn and came toward the house, causing Bud's wish to go unfinished.

3

"It's Uncle Jimmy Miller and 'Sody' Slavin," said Mrs. Daley.

"Two of the toughest old pelicans that ever wore a boot," remarked Bud as they rode up and dismounted.

Uncle Jimmy Miller was only five feet four inches tall, thin of frame, thin of voice, with whiskers of a gray old bob-cat and an explosive expression.

Sody Slavin was nearly six feet tall and so fat that he could hardly find a saddle-horse strong enough to carry him more than half a day at a time. Sody talked in a counter-tenor voice and panted at all times. He was of a nervous temperament and so ticklish that everything annoyed him. Uncle Jimmy owned the JM outfit – one of the big cattle outfits of the Modoc – and Sody was his foreman.

" 'Lo, Mrs. Daley," called Sody. "Nice weather we're havin'."

"Hallo, Mr. Slavin," she answered, smiling.

"Mister!" he snorted indignantly.

"Mrs.!" she shot right back at him.

"All right, May. I didn't want to call you May right in front of yore husband; but if you ain't scared of him, I ain't."

"That's what polite folks calls 'small-talk,' I reckon," observed Uncle Jimmy. "Anyway,

4

it's too darn small to pay for the wear and tear on yore teeth."

Uncle Jimmy spat dryly and turned to Bud.

"Well, whatcha know about it, Bud?"

"Not any more than I did before."

"Uh-huh." Uncle Jimmy scratched his moustache violently.

"Aw, they must 'a' strayed," said Sody. "Doggone it, yuh –"

"They did, like hell!" snorted Uncle Jimmy. "Sody, you ain't got – My gosh, you make me mad, Sody! Must' a' strayed! Since when did one brand of cows all git together and vamoose? Mebbe they didn't like to associate with the other brands, eh? Sody, you do think of the dangdest, craziest answers to questions."

"Mebbe I'm wrong," said Sody contritely.

"Mebbe!"

"You ain't got no better answer," grinned Sody. "They're all gone, ain't they? They must 'a' went away together."

"Yeah! With some range-burglars fannin' their south ends with a lariat."

Bud grinned in spite of his loss. To Uncle Jimmy and Sody Slavin, life was just one argument after another. At times the arguments grew so personal that Uncle Jimmy would fire Sody. He was known to have discharged Sody three times in one day, and Sody was known to have quit his job three times in one day. And the majority of their arguments were over things that neither of them knew anything about; which neither would admit.

"Well, let's not fight over it," said Bud. "They're gone, thasall."

"I know it," nodded Uncle Jimmy. "I know they're gone, Bud; but that – that –"

"Your Mister Slavin," suggested Sody sweetly.

"Yea-a-a-ah!" snorted Uncle Jimmy. "My mister!"

"What's the joke?" asked Bud.

"Joke, hell!" exploded Uncle Jimmy. "When Sody took that trip to 'Frisco he went out to a packin' plant. I s'pose he lied to 'em about the cows we've got out here, and all that. You know how a danged half-wit like him would talk. Anyway, I got a letter from the packer, and he says:

" 'Regardin' a conversation with your Mr. Slavin –'

"My Mister Slavin! He ain't mine, Bud. That's the only thing that saves him. If he was mine –"

"You wouldn't have to," interrupted Sody. "If I belonged to you, I'd 'a' grieved m'self to death long ago. There is things that flesh and blood can't stand."

6

"And you're one of 'em," declared Uncle Jimmy.

"If the argument is over, we might eat," smiled Mrs. Daley.

"It never was no argument, as far as I was concerned," said Uncle Jimmy. "I – I – Now, Sody, if you open your danged mouth, I'll –"

"Who's openin' their mouth?" demanded Sody. "You took exceptions to a statement I made, didn't yuh? Yeah, yuh did, too. I'll bet you don't even know what I said that started the argument."

"Don't I? The hell I don't! Huh! Do you?"

"Nope," said Sody honestly.

Uncle Jimmy stared at him for several moments, his moustache working violently. Then he turned his head and looked at Mrs. Daley, his face breaking into an expansive smile.

"May, you sure do look fine," he observed sincerely. "If I was thirty years younger, I'd sure steal yuh away from that good-for-nothing husband of yours."

Mrs. Daley laughed lightly, but Bud's laugh was bitter, as he unbuckled and kicked off his chaps.

"They've stole everythin' else from me, Uncle Jimmy."

"Yeah, that's true, I reckon."

Uncle Jimmy turned and squinted

reflectively at the sunswept hills of Modoc-land.

"Yeah, they've plumb cleaned yuh out, Bud. 'S far as I can see, yuh ain't got hide nor horn in this county. We've been free of rustlin' for a long time in the Modocs; but every once in a while they steps out and starts in where they left off. But I don't sabe it yet – nossir. Mebbe I've lost a few head – I dunno."

"But I've lost everything," said Bud. "I've worked awful hard to make this ranch pay, Uncle Jimmy. It ain't so much for myself as it is for May. She's had a lot of faith in me, and I wanted to give her things, but the cards broke against me."

"Aw, you can make it all back, Bud," assured the old man.

Bud smiled bitterly and shook his head.

"Sounds fine, Uncle Jimmy. I owe more money than I can ever pay back. It would take me a long time if things had broke right, but now –"

"I dunno," Uncle Jimmy scratched his head. "It don't look reasonable for anybody to plumb clean yuh out like this, but it's a cinch that there's no Triangle-D cattle in the Modoc hills."

"How does May take it?" asked Sody cautiously.

"She hasn't had time to realise what it

8

means. I planned to buy her a lot of new clothes and all them things that a woman wants. Oh, it's tough, boys! I reckon" – bitterly – "there's nothin' left for me to do, except to go out and stick up a treasure box."

"Hush up that stuff!" snorted Uncle Jimmy. "It ain't that bad."

"I was only jokin'. It takes nerve to steal – and my nerve is all gone."

"No, it ain't," denied Sody. "If you wanted to stick up a –"

"You'd help him, I suppose," finished Uncle Jimmy.

"I'd go into anythin' that's a payin' proposition."

"Go ahead, but keep out of this argument, Sody."

"May jist said that dinner was waitin'," reminded Sody.

"Well, who said she didn't?" demanded Uncle Jimmy. "You're always tryin' to start an argument, Sody."

"No such danged thing!" Sody shook his head violently. "I never start arguments, Jim. You start 'em, and then –"

"Let's eat," suggested Bud.

Thus ended another argument that might have lasted several minutes – and ended nowhere.

CHAPTER II

The Fall round-up of the Modoc country had just been completed, and in all those thousands of cattle there was not a single one bearing Bud Daley's Triangle-D brand. It was unbelievable, but true. An army of cowboys had ridden for days, combing the hills so thoroughly that hardly an animal had escaped them.

And all of them knew that Bud Daley owned at least five hundred head of cattle, outside of possible increase. Bud had been foreman for Uncle Jimmy Miller for a year; a top-hand cow-man, who had gained the respect of every one during that one year.

But Bud was not content with a salary. He had married May Lloyd, the prettiest girl in the Red Hills range country, and he wanted to make good for her sake. For a few hundred dollars he had acquired the Triangle ranch and iron, which he had had registered as the Triangle D. Bud had a little money which he invested in stock, starting his little herd.

Then he had gone to Cleve Lavelle, the political and cattle power of the Modoc country, and borrowed five thousand dollars, which he invested in cattle – or rather, all except two hundred dollars. Bud was a gambler. As soon as his cattle buying was over he went into the Rest Ye All gambling-house, which was owned by Cleve Lavelle, and won ten thousand dollars at roulette.

But, instead of paying Lavelle the borrowed money, he went out and bought cattle with every cent of it. This gave him a respectable-sized herd, and, barring the unforeseen, Bud Daley was destined to become a regular cattleman.

Cleve Lavelle came in for a great amount of good-natured joking over the fact that Bud had cleaned out the gambling-house, but Lavelle was a cool-nerved gambler and merely smiled. It was all in the game. Perhaps he felt that Bud should have paid his debts, but did not say so. Lavelle was close-mouthed, and his square, deep-lined face, thin lips and level gray eyes told nothing.

Lavelle owned the 76-A cattle outfit, located about six miles from the town of Modoc, where he employed a big crew of cowboys and broncho-riders. Lavelle broke many horses for the Eastern markets and took pride in the fact that he had the hardest riding crew of punchers in the county.

And Lavelle was the political power in Modoc County. He was a mixer, known as a square-shooter, but the political pot of the county was mixed in Lavelle's private office at the rear of the ornate Rest Ye All gambling-house in Modoc. Whether or not the ingredients were according to the pure political ideas of some of the people, they were according to Cleve Lavelle.

Bud Daley had not the slightest idea of who had taken his stock. If he had, he would not have gone to see Dug Breed, the sheriff, the day after the close of the round-up. Bud did not like Dug Breed. He had opposed Dug at the election of the year before and Dug had not forgotten it. He was a square-built man, about forty years of age, with harsh features, narrow lips and eyes that flashed green in anger.

Breed was a competent officer, saying little, drinking none and paying strict attention to running the sheriff's office. To him went Bud. He had heard of Bud's loss. Every one on the Modoc range knew of it. Breed had little to say, but Bud felt that he did not believe that the stock had been stolen.

"You ain't sold any stock lately, have you, Daley?" he asked.

"Sold any?" Bud shook his head, and it suddenly dawned upon him that the sheriff was hinting that he had sold his stock and was trying to claim that he had been robbed.

For a moment he had difficulty in holding his temper.

"Mebbe," said the sheriff suggestively, "they were herded out through the Crooked Cañon country and shipped from Black Wells."

The Crooked Cañon country lay to the west of Bud's ranch, and Black Wells was a small shipping point thirty miles from Modoc. Before the advent of the railroad into Modoc, Black Wells had been the shipping point for all of the Modoc range.

"That's probably where they went," admitted Bud slowly, "and Black Wells ain't a place where yuh can get reliable information."

"No, it's a pretty safe place," said the sheriff thoughtfully, "folks over there mind their own business. This kinda leaves you in a bad shape, don't it, Daley?"

"Well," Bud smiled a trifle, "I've still got my health and the Triangle-D ranch."

"I mean – you're kinda left in debt, ain't yuh?"

"Am I?" Bud's lips shut tightly for a moment. "Where did yuh get that idea, Breed?"

"It ain't an idea, Daley. In fact, it's none of my business; but everybody knows that you couldn't accumulate a herd of that size in a

13

year and not be in debt. I hope you're not.
And if you are, I hope that yuh won't be stuck
for a payment."

"Stuck for it?"

"You know what I mean – have the ranch
taken away from yuh."

Bud laughed softly as he rolled a cigarette.
The ranch-house, brand, and the water-rights
to a few springs had cost him less than
five hundred dollars. The repairs would not
amount to more than two hundred more.

"You were just gettin' a good start,"
observed the sheriff.

Bud threw away his match and looked
quizzically at the sheriff.

"Breed, I didn't come here for sympathy,"
he said slowly. "If that's what I wanted, God
knows I'd never come to you. I've been
robbed, dontcha understand? Ain't it kinda
up to you to do something besides settin'
there and feelin' sorry for me?"

Breed frowned heavily for a moment,
looking down at the toes of his boots. Bud
turned away and moved over to the open door.
He had not expected much from Breed; so he
was not disappointed.

"Did you think I was offerin' you
sympathy?" asked Breed.

"I hoped you wasn't," said Bud, without
turning his head.

"Well, I wasn't." Breed laughed shortly and turned back to some papers on his desk.

Bud turned and looked at Breed, but the latter did not look up. For a moment Bud's lips curled with anger, and he rubbed an itching palm across the brass heads of the cartridges in his belt. He knew that Breed was a fighter, a dangerous man to provoke; yet every drop of fighting blood in his body cried out against the injustice of an officer refusing assistance because of a personal grudge.

But he fought down the desire to tell Breed what he thought of him and to back up his opinions with hot lead. Bud knew that one of them would probably never walk out of the place – possibly both. If the sheriff killed him, it would be easy to explain, but if he killed the sheriff – that would be a difficult situation.

So he turned, stepped out on the sidewalk, and crossed the street to the Rest Ye All saloon. It was the slack time of the day, and he found Cleve Lavelle in his private office reading a newspaper.

Lavelle put the paper aside, motioned Bud to a chair, and waited for him to speak.

"You heard what happened to me, didn't yuh, Lavelle?" asked Bud.

Lavelle nodded curtly. He did not seem greatly concerned.

"I'm broke, I reckon," continued Bud.

15

"Somebody has cleaned me out as slick as a rifle-barrel."

"I heard about it," said Lavelle. "Well?"

"Well?" Bud swallowed hard and shifted his position. "Well, I'm broke, thasall. I owe you five thousand dollars, Lavelle."

"You do."

"Due next month," said Bud.

"The first of the month, Daley."

"All right. It looks to me like it was just too bad, thasall."

"You can't pay it?" Coldly.

"What with?"

"Mm-m-m." Lavelle rubbed his chin with a hand that was just a trifle over-decorated with diamonds. Bud estimated that just one of those white stones would cost more than his debt.

"What's your ranch worth, Daley?" asked Lavelle.

"That's a question," replied Bud thoughtfully. "It ain't for sale."

"Possibly not," smiled Lavelle, "but under the present situation, I might have to take it over."

"I reckon I get yore idea," nodded Bud, "but I didn't come with that idea in mind a-tall Lavelle. Yuh see, it's like this: yo're a gambler, Lavelle. You ain't got a ghost of a chance to ever get that five thousand. My

16

ranch ain't worth a fifth of that amount."

"I understand that!" snapped Lavelle.

"You've set into big games," continued Bud, ignoring the interruption. "You've been stuck for five thousand dollars lots of times. Did you quit, Lavelle?"

"What do you mean?"

"Did you quit the game, when you was five thousand in it?"

"No." Lavelle shook his head. "No, I never quit, but –"

"Yo're into my game five thousand dollars, Lavelle. If you quit now, you lose five thousand; if you back me again, you've got a chance to get yore money back."

"Like hell I have!" Lavelle threw back his head and laughed. "Daley, you've got more nerve than a bank robber. Do you think I'd gamble at those odds?"

Bud did not laugh. His blue eyes bored into Lavelle's face, and his jaw was set tight.

"You sure make me laugh," declared Lavelle.

"Ten thousand dollars would put me on my feet, Lavelle," persisted Bud. "Inside of three years –"

"They'd clean you out again," finished Lavelle. "Now you've got me all wrong, Daley. On the first of next month, you be here with five thousand dollars."

17

Lavelle dropped a heavy fist on the polished surface of his desk.

"In the first place, I don't think that anybody robbed you. It isn't reasonable, Daley. Look at the thing right."

Bud got to his feet and stood looking down at Lavelle.

"Just what do you mean by that remark, Lavelle?"

"Figure it out for yourself, Daley."

"You mean that I —"

Bud leaned forward, his hands clenched tightly as he stared down at Lavelle.

"Hold your temper," advised Lavelle. "You're not a good bluffer, Daley."

"I'm not goin' to bluff," said Bud slowly. "I'm goin' to mean everythin' I say to you, Lavelle. Yo're —"

"Wait a moment," interrupted Lavelle. "You are going to say something that you'll be sorry for, Daley. You already owe me more than you want to pay, and you are sore because I won't lend you more. Your opinions of me are of no interest to any one, except yourself; so tell them to yourself and save trouble."

Bud relaxed slowly and a grin wreathed his lips. Then he laughed and turned to the door.

"All right, Lavelle. I reckon that's good
18

advice. I'm sorry I acted like a fool, and I'll try to have that money for yuh."

Bud crossed the gambling room and entered the bar, where he found Sody Slavin and "Dinah" Blewette. Dinah was a little dark-skinned cowpuncher from the JM ranch, with an impediment in his speech, bow-legs, and a totally bald head.

They greeted Bud effusively and expansively. Between them they owned the world and were perfectly willing to cut their share to thirds. Would he accept?

"I ain't a bit dry," protested Bud. "Not a danged bit, boys."

"Bud's had grief," explained Sody, while Dinah listened attentively. "He's sure had flocks of grief, Dinah."

"Sh-sure," agreed Dinah, nodding violently, which caused his sombrero to shift in a circle on his bald dome.

"I – I – I – I – I –"

"That's all from you," interrupted Sody. "Me and Bud will do all the talkin', Dinah. Thasall right, we'll excuse yuh from participatin' in conversation. You nod or shake, thasall."

Dinah's lips worked convulsively for a moment, as if trying to frame a protest; but he broke into an expansive grin and turned to the bar, signalling

19

frantically for the bartender to show more speed.

Bud could not resist their invitation. It had been a long time since he had taken a drink, and the potent liquor lifted him out of his blue haze and transported him into a world which was filled with rose-tinted atmosphere.

Lavelle came through the bar-room a little later, but none of the three cowboys paid any attention to him. Other cowboys, with their round-up stakes in their pockets, were invading the place, anxious for their drinks and a chance to woo the Goddess of Luck.

"She's goin' to be a big night," declared Sody. "A big night."

"Yuh – yuh – yuh – yuh –" choked Dinah.

"Yuh betcha," said Sody, anticipating what Dinah was trying to say. "Now, you stop that, Dinah. Yo're a good cowboy and I like yuh fine; but you never was intended to talk."

"Tha – tha – tha – tha –"

"That's right," prompted Bud, nodding violently. "We know all about yuh, Dinah." And then to Sody, "I'll make yuh a little bet that Dinah can't say 'Piper Heidsick' inside of five minutes."

"Not with me, yuh don't," grinned Sody. "The last time he tried to say it, he was plumb unconscious for an hour. My gosh, he jist chokes plumb to death. Uncle Jimmy wanted

20

him to bring some chewin' tobacco one day. Uncle Jimmy chaws Piper; so he tells Dinah to bring him some. 'Shorty' Ryan was workin' out there at that time, and he chaws Star. He wanted some too.

"Well, Dinah comes down to the store and horns up to the counter. He was goin' to order the Star first. They tells me that he started to siss-s-s – You know what I mean? Well, he keeps it up for so long that everybody thought he was loaded to the gills with sody water. Dinah sees that it ain't goin' to be no success; so he decides to buy the Piper Heidsick first.

"Well, I reckon the change didn't do Dinah no good, 'cause he collapsed before he ever got past the pup part of it."

Dinah took it good-naturedly, but tried for the next fifteen minutes to tell Bud that Sody's story was a darn lie. Bud knew what Dinah wanted to say; so everybody was satisfied. Things were going along fine, until some of the 4-A cowboys came in, loaded for bear.

Among them was "Short-Horn" Adams, a fat-faced, blear-eyed puncher, who had in some way incurred the displeasure of Dinah Blewette. Dinah was getting all tuned to sing a song, when he happened to see Short-Horn. Dinah proceeded to swing his heavy beer glass overhanded and threw it with all his strength at his enemy.

It was a good shot – except that Dinah threw it at Short-Horn's reflection in the back-bar mirror, causing the big mirror to radiate cracks in every direction and creating havoc among the stacks of glittering glassware on the backbar.

Dug Breed happened to be among those present and proceeded to collar the luckless Dinah, who was but a handful for Breed. As a result of his reverse-English marksmanship Dinah would have probably spent the night in Modoc jail, but about that time Sody Slavin accidentally tangled his feet with those of Dug Breed, and the sheriff sat down hard.

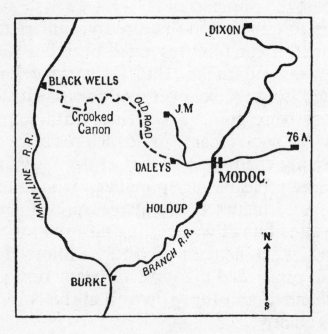

And Dinah ducked like a rabbit, although a trifle uncertain of gait, while the cow-punchers cheered everybody concerned. Breed got to his feet, blazing with wrath, only to be met with words of apology and regret from Sody Slavin.

"My gosh, that was awful," explained Sody. "I dunno how in the devil m' feet ever got over there."

Sody seemed very sincere and serious. Breed glared at him, his fists clenched tightly at his sides. There was no doubt that the sheriff was fighting mad.

But Sody ignored the sheriff's attitude as he kept on explaining:

"I must 'a' slipped, don'tcha know it? I'm sure-footed too. I must 'a' stepped on somethin' with m' left foot, and m' right swung like this."

Sody's exaggerated slip caused him to lose balance and his swinging right foot caught Breed on the shin-bone of his right leg. It was a painful thing. Sody was badly off balance; so he grabbed at the yelping sheriff and they both went down, half under a table, with Sody on top.

The fall half stunned Breed, but did not affect Sody, who got to his feet, still apologising and dragged his spurred heel across the sheriff's kneecaps as he stepped

23

away. Breed struggled to his feet and leaned on the table, panting and cursing painfully. He was so mad that his eyes were shut.

Then Bud blundered into the table, knocking away the sheriff's visible means of support; and he and Sody went out through the front door. They heard the sheriff hit the floor again, and his curses were wonderful to hear; but Sody and Bud were too joyful to care about mere words.

"Oh, m'gawd!" wheezed Sody, clinging to Bud. "It went jist like clockwork, Bud. Ain't I the thinker? Ain't I? And then you moved the table away from him! Ha-ha-ha-ha-ha!"

"He'll try to kill us both," choked Bud.

"He can't. It's ag'in the law, Bud."

"He's so mad that the law won't stop him, Sody."

"All right," laughed Sody. "I hope I don't die so painful that I can't take time to think of how I kicked him in the shin, fell on top of him and then spurred him in the knee. Ha-ha-ha! And every danged bit of it was accidental, too."

"I couldn't help bumpin' into that table," added Bud. "I was so drunk I never knowed what I was doin'. I wonder where Dinah went?"

"He won't go far," gasped Sody. "What did the darn fool bust that mirror for? Why, he just whaled away at it with his glass."

"I – I – I – I – I –"

Dinah stepped out from the dark corner of the building and began his explanation.

"Wait a minute," begged Sody. "Let's get farther away from Breed."

They went farther down the street and stopped in a dark spot.

"Didja jist want to bust that mirror?" asked Sody. "Don't talk, Dinah; nod or shake."

Dinah shook.

"Accidental?"

Dinah shook again.

"Uh-huh," reflected Sody. "Tha's funny."

"Say, didja see somebody in the mirror?"

Dinah nodded violently.

"Who?" asked Sody.

"Sh – sh – sh – sh – sh –"

"Stop it!" snapped Sody. "Was it Short-Horn Adams?"

Dinah nodded quickly.

"Well, that's settled," said Sody. "Now what do we do?"

"I'm goin' home," said Bud. "I've got a home and a wife, yuh must remember."

"If I was in yore condition, I'd not thank anybody to remind me of it," said Sody seriously. "You might as well stay and make a good night of it, Bud."

25

"I'll be sober by the time I get home, Sody."

"Yeah – by the time yuh git home. You'll prob'ly fall off yore horse before yuh get there."

"No, I won't, either. You and Dinah better go home, too. If yuh stay around here, Breed'll have yuh both in jail."

"You better stay," insisted Sody. "You'll get a lot of good laughs out of watchin' him try it."

But Bud had made up his mind to go home; so Dinah and Sody parted reluctantly with him and went seeking more fun, while Bud mounted and rode swiftly out of Modoc.

CHAPTER III

It was five miles from town to Bud's ranch, but before he had gone half the distance he realised that he contained far too much whisky. Solitude and the swinging motion of his horse caused him to realise also that he was in no condition to converse with his wife.

"It can't last always," he told himself; "so I'll swing into the hills and ride it off."

There was a full moon, which lighted the hills, and a cool breeze that fanned his fevered brow; but instead of sobering up, he grew even more intoxicated. In a half-daze he circled through the hills and came in at the rear of the ranch.

He could see a dim light in the living-room, and he knew that May was waiting up for him. He felt sorry for her. He had promised her many things which she had been denied, now he was worse than broke. He remembered dimly that Breed was not going to try to find the stolen cattle, and that Lavelle had refused to help him again. It seemed like weeks ago that he had talked with them. He dismounted and dropped the reins, forgetting to unsaddle his horse.

"To heck with 'em!" he told himself thickly. "I'll git along. Tha's jist what I'll do – git along, y'betcha."

He approached the house from the rear, laughing foolishly at his erratic progress. At the kitchen door he stopped. The door was open. A foolish idea took root in his addled brain. He would take off his boots and sneak in. The idea appealed to him immensely.

So he sat down on the step and drew off his boots, chuckling to himself. Somewhere he had heard of a drunken man doing that same thing. It didn't seem so funny then, but it did now. Perhaps, he thought, May might be asleep – and never know that he did not come home sober.

He tucked a boot under each arm and crept inside. He could see the light in the living-room. It was an oil-lamp turned low. Into the living-room he went and stopped near the table. The front door, which led out on to a porch, was open, and he heard voices. They were talking softly.

Bud frowned and listened closely, but could not hear plainly enough; so he moved over closer to the door. It was a man's voice and a woman's. He could hear them plain enough now. The man's voice was very distinct:

"Oh, I know – loyalty and all that. But you've tried it two years. And what have you got? Nothing. Why, this ranch wouldn't bring the price of two dresses – the kind you ought to have."

Bud blinked wonderingly, straining his ears for the woman's reply, which was pitched too low for him to hear what she said. He looked around the room, as if wondering if he had entered the wrong house by mistake. Then the man's voice again:

"Look at it right. You are young yet; the prettiest woman in this county. Do you want to throw away your youth? Do you want to look like the rest of these cattlemen's wives in a few years, or do you want to live in luxury, retain your beauty?

"Bud Daley can never hope to give you much. I will admit that Bud is doing the best he can, but it isn't enough. As a cattleman, he is a failure; and you two can't live on a cowpuncher's salary. Just now," the man laughed, "he is down in Modoc filling his skin with whisky – leaving you here alone."

If the woman made any reply, Bud was unable to hear it. He was sober now. The whisky had evaporated from his brain. He looked down at his bedraggled socks and at the boots under his arms. He lifted his eyes and stared toward the door, as the man's voice continued:

"I remember when you came here to Modoc. I knew then that you were the most beautiful girl I had ever seen. I pictured you in silks and furs, May. Since then you have been in my dreams, day-dreams and night-dreams. You are not happy. No, you are not. Can you look me in the eyes and tell me that you are satisfied with life? No, I didn't think you could.

"May, you can't afford to throw away your life. Bud is man enough to understand – and if he doesn't – well, what matter?"

Bud's face had gone gray in the yellow light of the lamp, and the lines of his face deepened, as he stared across the room into space. His mouth was so dry that it was painful, and his eyes ached from the intensity of looking far into the future.

He braced his hand against the wall and tried to listen again. There was a throbbing noise in his ears, and he suddenly discovered that it was his own heart. The man was talking again, and his voice, low-pitched as it was, came clear to Bud's ears:

"May, you know I love you. You know I can give you everything in the world to make you happy. We'll go away from this country – go back east, where we can enjoy life. This isn't living."

Her reply was inaudible, but it seemed to awaken a new note in the man's arguments.

"Oh, I know all that, May. But no one can ever censure you for doing this. The world owes you happiness, little woman – and I think that fate sent me to you."

"Fate sent him," said Bud to himself, as though stating a great truth. "Fate sent him, thasall."

He nodded slowly. Suddenly he shoved away from the wall, a great rage welling up in his heart against this man who would steal his wife away; the man who came in the night, knowing that the husband was in Modoc – drunk.

30

His hand clenched around the butt of his six-shooter, and the hammer clicked softly under his thumb. The sound seemed to sober him, and he squinted down at the gun. He was going to kill a man now. He was going to walk out there and send a soul to eternity; the soul of a thief. He even laughed softly to himself, as he balanced the heavy gun. The voice of the man came again:

"You are entitled to happiness, May. Bud Daley can never make you happy."

The lines of Bud's face relaxed slowly and he stared at the gun. "Entitled to happiness," he repeated to himself. "Yeah, I suppose everybody is. If she can't be happy with me – and I kill him –" He shook his head slowly, as he replaced his gun.

"What happiness would I get through killin' him?" he wondered. "Mebbe I'd kill her happiness. God, this is a funny world you made. I dunno what to do now, but I've got to quit listenin'."

They were talking again, but he did not listen. The world had gone flat, stale. He wondered dimly if May had a wrap around her shoulders. It was cool out there on the porch. He felt cold.

Then he found himself back at his horse and started to mount before he realised that he still carried his boots. They were hard to get on, and he wondered why he had ever taken them off. It was a foolish thing to do, he thought.

He mounted his horse and looked slowly around.

"Where am I goin'?" he asked himself, half aloud. "I'm ready to go, and there ain't no place."

Somewhere a cow bawled sleepily.

"Wish I was a cow," said Bud wearily. "Cows don't think."

On all sides stretched the moonlit hills, silver, blue and haze that hid their harsh outlines – a sparkling fairyland, topped with a ceiling of stars. Bud turned and rode out of the rear gate, heading into the hills; riding away from humanity, seeking the open spaces to clear his brain.

On the slope of the hill he drew rein and looked back toward the ranch-house, where the oil-lamp gleamed, a dull pin-point of yellow light. It seemed that he could still hear the drone of voices on the front porch; but it was only the whispering of the breeze through the purple sage.

"Lavelle, I reckon yo're right," he said softly. "Bud Daley can't ever hope to give her much. And she can't afford to throw away her life – look like the rest of the cattlemen's wives. I – I never thought about it thataway, Lavelle."

Bud sighed deeply and the fumes of the forgotten whisky tasted sour to his palate.

"Gawd," he said softly, "you made a wonderful world, but, if I'm any judge, the makin' of humanity wasn't no job for one man."

Then he bowed his head and rode straight into the hills.

CHAPTER IV

After Bud had left them, Sody and Dinah proceeded to keep out of Dug Breed's way and to drink much liquor. Dinah promised Sody that he would bury the hatchet as far as Short-Horn Adams was concerned and hold nothing but good thoughts for everybody.

And so passed several pleasant hours in the lives of Dinah and Sody. The wooden sidewalks became far too narrow for their tread and the buildings, at times, surged and jerked violently. Then, without any warning, Dinah's cup of joy turned sour, and he choked with a great emotion. In fact, he wept brokenly. Sody tried to cheer him, without avail. Then a great sadness came down upon Sody, and he cried too.

It is very likely that the tears blinded them to such an extent that they separated. No one will ever know whether Sody lost Dinah or Dinah lost Sody. Anyway, as soon as he partly recovered from his crying spree, Sody went hunting for his little partner.

But in all that vast army of gyrating houses, lamps, cowboys, he was unable to find the object of his search. From saloon to saloon he went, but there was no sign of Dinah Blewette. Then Sody decided that Dinah had gone home; so he went to the hitch-rack, intending to see if Dinah's horse was still there.

It was – and so was Dinah. He was sitting on the ground, with his back up against a post, and Sody did not see him until he stepped on his leg.

"Yuh-yuh-yuh –" began Dinah indignantly.

"Oh, there yuh are, eh?" said Sody.

Sody lighted a match and looked Dinah over. His eyes were swollen and purple, his nose slightly out of line, and he appeared to be minus several front teeth. Taking him all in all, Dinah was a greatly changed man.

"Yuh found Short-Horn, didn't yuh," commented Sody. "Don't try to answer me,

Dinah. Every inch of yuh proclaims the fact that you cried yor way into his heart. My gawd, but yo're a mess!"

He helped Dinah to his feet and backed him against the post, while he tried to wipe Dinah's face with a handkerchief, which only increased the misery of the little cowpuncher.

"Don't try to tell me what to do," growled Sody. "Yore face has got to be set right, or it'll look awful queer. You ain't got no sense, Dinah. Short-Horn is big enough to tie yuh in a knot and hang yuh up to dry."

"He-he dud-did," said Dinah sadly.

"Uh-huh." Sody made a last swipe at Dinah's face with the handkerchief and hitched up his own belt.

"Well, we'll have speech with Mister Short-Horn, Dinah. He's a powerful mean critter, the same of which I ain't too drunk to remember; so I goes cautious-like. I ain't takin' yore troubles upon me, yuh understand. Yore battles are yore battles, Dinah; but jist now I feels antagonistic agin' him and all his ilk.

"Know what 'ilk' means, Dinah? Don't answer me. My gosh, I do like these one-sided conversations. C'mon."

Sody hitched up his belt, squared around to get his bearings and headed for the Rest Ye All, with Dinah weaving along in his wake.

35

For all of his huge bulk, Sody was as hard as nails; but he was cognizant of the fact that he was just a little too drunk to do a good job of fighting with his hands.

The Rest Ye All was well filled with cowboys, who were spending their round-up stakes as fast as possible. The long bar was crowded to capacity, and the gambling-hall, at the rear, was blue with tobacco smoke and shifting forms. Sody shouldered his way past the bar, with Dinah following along in his wake, taking advantage of Sody's bulk to clear a trail for him.

Dug Breed was coming out into the bar-room, elbowing his way along; but when he saw Sody and Dinah he turned around and forced his way back. Breed had heard that Short-Horn Adams had whipped Dinah Blewette, and he knew that the trail of these two JM cowpunchers would probably lead to trouble.

And not only that, but Breed held no forgiveness in his heart for what Sody had done to him earlier in the evening; and he was all primed to tap Sody over the head with a gun and take him to jail.

Short-Horn Adams was bucking a roulette wheel at the extreme end of the room and was having no luck whatever. Short-Horn's voice was plainly audible as he complained over his ill-luck. Other punchers laughed, shouted with rough glee and placed their bets.

A dapper little gambler was running the game, his derby hat cocked at a rakish angle on his head, a cigar held jauntily between his teeth. Short-Horn glared belligerently at him, as the gambler raked in Short-Horn's last bets.

"The house is lucky to-night, gents," he laughed. "Put down your contributions and accept our sympathy."

"Yeah, yo're sure lucky," agreed Short-Horn. "I betcha I know what makes yuh lucky."

With a sweep of his hand, Short-Horn removed the hat from the gambler's head and placed it on his own. Short-Horn's head was a trifle too small and the derby fitted down over his brows.

"Now spin yore wheel," roared Short-Horn. "C'mon, gents. I've removed the curse from our midst, and we c'n break the danged game in three whirls."

Whap!

Sody's broad palm descended upon the derby with great force and drove it down over Short-Horn's head, covering his face and wedging it down over his ears. Short-Horn whirled around clawing at the brim of the hat, but only succeeding in ripping the brim away.

37

"Now yuh got him, Dinah," said Sody calmly. "He's yore size now, li'l' feller. Help yoreself to the mustard."

And Dinah did not need a second invitation. With both fists he hammered the blinded Short-Horn unmercifully, while the crowd cheered wildly and gave him plenty of room. Many of them knew that Short-Horn had beaten Dinah, and they wanted to see the smaller man even the score, even if he was doing it unfairly.

While Short-Horn clawed at the hat-brim, which stuck tightly, Dinah socked him with both fists, driving him back into the roulette layout. And then, through the cheering crowd, came Dug Breed, shoving his way to the centre, only to be met by Sody Slavin.

"Stop it!" yelped Breed, "I'll arrest every –"

But his threat was unfinished, when Sody bumped into him, crashing him back into the crowd. At this moment, Short-Horn managed to get the hat loose, and charged Dinah, who ducked down and let Short-Horn fall over him.

"Rattle yore hocks, Dinah!" yelled Sody. "The sheriff is angry with us. C'mon!"

Sody dived straight at the crowd, with Dinah wobbling after him, and the crowd surged in behind them, blocking the sheriff and the cruising Short-Horn, who had a gun in his hand and murder in his eye.

Straight out past the bar went Sody and Dinah, heading for their horses, which were up the street at the nearest hitch-rack. Sody knew that it would be dangerous for them to stay in Modoc. It would mean a gun-battle with Short-Horn and his gang – if the sheriff did not get them first.

They had swung on to their horses and spurred into the street when they heard the unmistakable thud of a revolver shot, fired from inside a building. Sody's horse lurched sidewise and went to its knees, while Sody flung himself free, bounced to his feet, and ran to Dinah, who was having trouble with his animal.

Up behind Dinah's saddle climbed the big cowpuncher, while Dinah's horse, unused to a double load, bawled wildly, threw down its head and bucked out of town, heading for the home ranch.

But the bucking was of short duration, because of the fact that Sody's weight was too much for the broncho to handle; but they faded out of Modoc's sight so fast that only a wisp of dust blew back to show of their leaving.

Dug Breed clawed his way to the street about the time that they faded out. Several others arrived about this time, their interest centred on Sody's horse, which sprawled in the middle of the street. The fact that some one had fired several pistol shots did not alarm them in the least.

"I heard three shots fired," volunteered a cowpuncher. "I was comin' up the street and I see this horse go down. I think the first shot hit the horse, but I dunno where they was fired from."

Dug Breed said nothing. The horse was quite dead; so they unsaddled it, and two cowboys, using their ropes, hooked on to it from their saddle-horns and dragged the carcass off the street.

Breed knew that the shots had not been fired by Short-Horn nor by any one in the Rest Ye All; and he wondered who else had a grievance against Sody Slavin.

Across the street was a general merchandise store, post office, restaurant, and the Modoc bank. The restaurant was the only one of the four that was open at this time of night. Farther up that side of the street were more saloons, but the shots could hardly have been fired from there.

Beside the Rest Ye All saloon was a big feed store on one side, and on the other was another general merchandise store, both closed. Breed found the cowboy who had heard the shots and questioned him.

"I dunno much about it," confessed the cowboy, "but they did not seem to come from the other side, and they was kinda muffled, like they was from inside a house. I heard one shot, and then I seen the horse fall down. I was kinda interested in that, but I sure heard two more shots."

Breed crossed the street and walked past the restaurant. There were several diners within, busily engaged with their food. He walked past the store, which was unlighted, the door locked. The post office was locked, blinds drawn.

But in front of the Modoc bank he stopped. There was glass on the sidewalk, which had fallen from one of the front windows. A closer examination showed that almost the entire pane was missing.

"Did somebody shoot from inside the bank?" wondered Breed, as he peered in through the broken window.

He broke away some of the jagged glass and prepared to climb within, but changed his mind. It might look bad, he thought.

It was only a short distance to the home of Frank Jordan, the president of the bank, and Breed negotiated it in short order.

Jordan was asleep, but Breed beat a tattoo on the door with the muzzle of his gun and soon aroused him.

41

"This is the sheriff," informed Breed. "One of the front windows of the bank has been smashed out."

"Smashed out?" Jordan grew very wide awake. "Who smashed it?"

"I dunno!" snapped Breed. "Hop into yore pants and let's find out. And don't forget yore key."

Jordan appeared in a few minutes, and they hurried down to the bank. Breed told him nothing about the shots nor of the dead saddle-horse, but Jordan volunteered the information that George Findlay, the cashier, intended to work late that evening.

"Did he have anythin' agin' Sody Slavin?" asked Breed.

"Slavin? That big cowboy? Why, I – I really can't say, sheriff. Not that I know of. In fact, I doubt that George knows him."

Jordan grunted wonderingly at the broken window and opened the door. The bank was lighted with oil lamps, which it took several moments to find in the dark. The vault door was wide open, as was the inner door.

Jordan gawped wildly around, while Breed walked to the vault door and peered inside.

"Look over there!" exclaimed Jordan, pointing back toward the door.

Just to the left of the door, directly below the smashed window, was the huddled body of the bank cashier. Breed went swiftly to him, turning his face up to the light.

"Is he dead?" asked Jordan hoarsely.

"Yeah." Breed squinted at the window and back at the dead cashier.

"He's been hit over the head," said Breed. "Mebbe that didn't stop him; so they used lead on the poor devil. Better take a look at the vault, Jordan."

They left the body lying there and went to the vault, carrying a lamp. Swiftly the banker examined the place, but shook his head wearily.

"I can't tell how much, if anything, is missing, sheriff. It will take a complete check to tell. I am afraid that the Modoc bank is hit hard."

He stooped and picked up several loose bills which had been dropped on the floor. The sheriff picked up several silver dollars, and among them was a silver piece, which was not a dollar. He looked closely at it.

"What is it, sheriff?" asked the banker.

"A rosette," said Breed thoughtfully.

"A rosette?"

"Yeah. One of them ornaments that punchers wear on the side of their chaps. I'll keep this, 'cause it might come in handy."

They went back into the room, and the banker closed the vault, while Breed studied the case. There was a spot of blood on the floor near the vault door. The cashier was wearing a coat. Just to the right of the front door, the sheriff picked up a black hat.

"That's George's hat," said the banker.

"They probably laid for him," said Breed. "When he came out the door they herded him back in here, made him open the vault and then sapped him over the head. They probably thought he was hit hard enough to make him lay still; but he recovered and tried to make a getaway. They missed him with one shot and smashed the window. That bullet killed Sody Slavin's horse. The other two got George. You stay here while I get the coroner, Jordan."

"Have you any idea who did it?" asked Jordan.

"If I have, I ain't yellin' it," said Breed, and slammed the door behind him.

He felt of the hammered silver rosette as he hurried along, and the feel of it brought a grin to his lips.

CHAPTER V

It was after nine o'clock the following morning when Bud Daley rode up to his stable. All night long he had ridden the hills, and his horse stumbled wearily to a standstill, its head hanging.

And Bud was just as weary as the horse. His face was gray and drawn from his mental battle, but his lips were drawn tightly in a stern resolution to put the case squarely up to his wife. He felt that he would know in a moment just how she felt about it.

She came out through the kitchen door as he dismounted, shading her eyes from the sun, and walked slowly toward him, while he yanked the saddle from his horse.

Another rider was coming in toward the ranch, and Mrs. Daley turned to look at him. It was Dug Breed, the sheriff. He raised his hat to Mrs. Daley and dismounted beside her, as Bud came up to them.

"Hello, Dug," said Bud wearily.

He felt that Breed was out there because of what happened the night before, and grinned slightly as he remembered that he had knocked the table away from the sheriff.

"Mornin', Bud," said Breed, softly. "Been ridin'?"

Bud looked at his wife. Her general appearance indicated that she had spent a sleepless night. Breed looked at Bud's horse, which was rolling in the dust beside the corral. It was easy to see that the horse had travelled many miles during the night.

"Yeah," Bud nodded slowly. "I've been ridin'. Why?"

"Where yuh been ridin' to, Bud?"

"What's that to you, Dug?"

"Mebbe a lot – mebbe a little, Bud. Can yuh prove where you've been ridin'?"

Bud shifted uneasily and his eyes hardened.

"Where was you about midnight, Bud?" asked Breed.

"None of your blamed business!"

Bud's body tensed angrily and his right hand dropped to his side. Mrs. Daley looked from one to the other quickly and started to put her hand on Bud's arm, but he stepped aside.

"I ain't goin' to quarrel with yuh, Bud," said Breed slowly. "You don't have to tell me where you've been, if yuh don't want to. But, under the circumstances, I've got to arrest yuh for the murder of George Findlay and for robbin' the Modoc bank."

Bud's right hand came up slowly and the

back of it brushed across his eyes. He scowled thoughtfully, but a grin crossed his lips.

"You jokin' me, Dug?" he asked hoarsely.

"Wish I was, Bud. You'll come peaceful like, won't yuh?"

"I'm under arrest?"

"Yeah, yuh sure are, Bud. I hate –"

"What do you know about hate?" Bud's voice was flat, toneless.

He looked at his wife. Her eyes were wide with fright and her face looked pale and drawn.

"Bud," she whispered, "you – you didn't do this. Why, you couldn't have done a thing like that, Bud."

Bud looked at her thoughtfully. Then he shook his head, and a wistful smile passed his lips as he said:

"May, yuh never can tell what a human bein' will do. I've kinda lost faith in folks."

"But you can prove that you didn't do it, can't you, Bud?"

"No-o-o," Bud shook his head. "I don't reckon I can, and I don't know anybody that can prove it for me."

Breed turned to Mrs. Daley.

"Wasn't Bud home last night?"

"You don't need to answer that, May," said Bud quickly.

"No, she don't have to," admitted Breed.

47

"But why do yuh blame me for it, Dug?" asked Bud. "You ain't told me a thing, except that I'm guilty."

Breed stepped in closer to Bud, examining the sides of his leather chaps, while Bud watched him curiously. Then Breed pointed to a spot about midway of Bud's right leg.

"Where's the rosette gone, Bud?"

"The rosette?"

Bud frowned and looked closely. On the left leg there were five silver rosettes; on the right there were only four. They were of a peculiar design, hand hammered from silver. Bud had made them from Mexican silver and had stamped the designs with a leather stamping tool.

"I must 'a' lost it," muttered Bud.

"I found it on the vault floor," said Breed slowly, watching Bud's face. "There was some scattered money, too. Findlay was over by the front window – dead."

"On the vault floor?" muttered Bud vacantly. "That's funny."

He examined the leg of his chaps closely. The piece of whang leather, which looped through the rosette, had worn through.

"Yeah – on the vault floor," said Breed.

"Oh, Bud!" breathed his wife. "You didn't do this. Say that you didn't do it, Bud!"

Bud sighed and shook his head.

48

"What's the use, May? I reckon it don't make much difference, anyway."

He held out his hands to Breed, a wistful smile on his lips.

"Better put 'em on, Dug, yuh never can tell about me – or any other human bein'."

Breed snapped the handcuffs on Bud's wrists, took Bud's gun and shoved it inside his own waistband.

"You'll have to saddle my horse for me, Dug," Bud grinned.

"All right," Breed sighed with relief.

He was glad to have taken Bud Daley without trouble. Bud followed him down to the horse, but Mrs. Daley turned and went back into the house, a dejected little figure, and leaned against the kitchen door wearily, while Bud and the sheriff rode away.

Bud did not look back.

"Mebbe it's better this way," he told himself. "I don't care a dang what happens from now on."

The sheriff and Bud were hardly out of sight when Sody and Dinah rode in from the JM. Mrs. Daley was sitting on the kitchen doorstep, her head buried in her hands, but looked up at sound of their horses.

"Mornin', Mrs. Daley," said Sody rather apologetically. "Me and Dinah kinda stopped in."

He didn't care to tell her that they had stopped to see if Bud had managed to get safely home from Modoc.

"Yes?" she said, and Sody noticed that her face was tear-stained.

"Didn't get home all right," he told himself, as he and Dinah exchanged glances. Sody wished he was somewhere else just now.

"Huh-huh-huh-how –" began Dinah, but Sody stopped him with –

"Don't do it, Dinah! You jist nod or shake; *sabe?*"

"Won't you get down?" asked Mrs. Daley.

"Sh-sh-sh-sh –" spluttered Dinah.

"Do it!" wailed Sody. "Mrs. Daley, I'm goin' to kill that jigger right in the middle of one of his speeches some day." He swung off his horse and dropped the reins.

"Bud home?" he asked.

Mrs. Daley shook her head, and the tears started again.

"He – he ain't sick, is he?" blurted Sody.

Mrs. Daley shook her head. "No, Sody; the sheriff just took him to jail."

"Oh, yeah!" Sody fought his hat for several seconds. "Well, that's funny. By golly, that's the first time he ever took Bud to jail. Huh! Now, Dinah, you relax yore mouth. That's right, cowboy. Kinda let down on yore vocal cords, too. Complete repose. Fine. Now,

50

control yoreself." He turned to Mrs. Daley and hitched up his belt.

"The sheriff was sore, was he?"

"No, I don't think he was sore."

"Yuh don't think he was? Huh! Well, that's funny."

Mrs. Daley evidently did not see the humour of the situation. She turned and went into the house, leaving Sody and Dinah staring at each other.

"Uh-uh-uh –" began Dinah.

"Aw-w-w-w, don't talk so much!" snapped Sody. "Me and you better go to town and see how we stand, Dinah. No, don't try to argue with me. Git on yore dignity and shut up. C'mon."

They rode away toward Modoc, wondering just what it all meant. Sody turned in his saddle.

"They can't jail yuh for bein' funny, Dinah."

"Ca-ca-ca –"

"No, they can't!"

There was no demonstration in Modoc when the sheriff came in with his prisoner. Bud was well liked by the cattlemen. Jordan had made an investigation of the robbery and found that the Modoc bank was about twenty thousand dollars the loser.

Jordan lost no time in interviewing Bud in the jail. Even if Bud was convicted, the fact still remained that the Modoc bank was still twenty thousand dollars short – which was a lot of money.

Jordan intimated that the return of the money would react in Bud's favour; but Bud only grinned at him and reminded him that murder was murder and had nothing whatever to do with money.

"And besides," reminded Bud, "if I was able to hand yuh back that money, it would only cinch the murder on to me. Whoever got that money killed Findlay."

Then came Uncle Jimmy Miller, like a raging bob-cat. He swore and raved about what he was going to do, while Bud grinned and smoked his cigarettes. Then he cooled down and told Bud that one of Bud's shots had killed Sody Slavin's horse. The fact that Uncle Jimmy was sure that Bud had done the job made no difference.

"I'll back yuh for the last damn cent I've got," he declared. "Never did have no use for banks, by gosh! Wanted to borrow some money about a year ago from Jordan. Wanted ten p'cent! Wanted me to give him a mortgage on the JM. Dang him, he wanted the world with a fence around it. Jist the same as told me that m' word wasn't no good. I'll betcha

52

he'll be dunnin' yuh for ten p'cent, if they convicts you, Bud."

"They'll likely hang me, if they find me guilty," grinned Bud.

"Like hell they will! Let 'em try it. By gosh I'll organise a gang of m' own and take this town apart. Oh, I ain't too old to act right smart at times, Bud. I used t' be a hellion in m' time, and Dug Breed won't be the first sheriff that I've called upon to hunt a new stompin'-ground. And some of 'em has sure hummed like a spike gettin' away, too."

Bud laughed and shook his head.

"Better let things go as they lay, Uncle Jimmy."

"Uh-huh." Thoughtfully. "What about May? How'd she take it?"

"Oh, all right, I reckon."

Uncle Jimmy considered Bud closely.

"You and May ain't antagonistic toward each other, are yuh?"

"No-o-o."

"Yes, yuh are. Now, you jist set easy, Bud; I'll take care of May."

Bud shook his head and stared at the ashes of his cigarette.

"Better let her alone, Uncle Jimmy."

"Thasso? You go to hell, will yuh?" Uncle Jimmy got to his feet and backed to the barred

53

door. "You see if I let her alone, young feller. Ain't either one of yuh got any sense? Now you set down on the seat of yore pants, 'cause you ain't goin' nowhere."

Dug Breed unlocked the door and Uncle Jimmy went swearing back to the streets.

Sody and Dinah came cautiously back to town, but every one seemed to have forgotten the incidents of the night before. Uncle Jimmy told them about the arrest, and Sody swore wonderingly at the fact that it was one of Bud's misdirected shots that killed his horse.

"Gug-gosh!" blurted Dinah in amazement.

"Now, that's about all from you," warned Sody. "This ain't a case that requires a lot of conversation, Dinah. How much money did Bud get, Uncle Jimmy?"

"Twenty thousand dollars."

"The ol' son of a gun!" applauded Sody. "Bud ain't no piker, is he? Whooee-e-e! Twenty thousand!"

"But he's in jail for murder," reminded Uncle Jimmy.

"I know, but – gosh, that's a lot of money. He likely planted it in a safe place, too."

"You kinda amaze me, Sody," said Uncle Jimmy sadly. "Don'tcha know yo're applaudin' a murderer? My gosh, ain'tcha got no respect for the law?"

"Since when did you git so danged sanitary?" demanded Sody.

"I've allus respected the law, Sody." Softly and sadly.

"You have, like hell!"

"I have respect for the law, Sody."

"Yeah, sure yuh have. You respect a kickin' bronc, too. You don't monkey with the business end of the darn thing; you get ahead of it."

"He-he-he-he," chuckled Dinah.

"Sure he does," interrupted Sody. "We know him. He gits ahead of the law – where the thing can't kick him. Ha-ha-ha-ha!"

"A prophet is without honour in his own home town," said Uncle Jimmy sadly, shaking his head.

"Profit!" snorted Sody. "Yo're a dead loss, Jim Miller. Let's go and git a drink."

"If I was in m' right mind, I'd fire you, Sody," declared Uncle Jimmy.

"If you wait for that, I've got a life job," grinned Sody.

They went into the Rest Ye All and stopped at the bar. Several men were there, and among them was Cleve Lavelle. He nodded absently and continued to converse with the others. Naturally the robbery and murder was the topic of conversation.

55

"I dunno how Bud Daley is goin' to even hire a lawyer," said one of the men. "He's flat broke, I hear."

"I'll be damned if he is!" snorted Uncle Jimmy, "the JM ranch is behind him, with every horn and hide I've got."

"You don't think he's guilty, Miller?" asked Lavelle.

"What the devil difference does that make?"

"All right," nodded Lavelle. "I'll go fifty-fifty with you on the deal."

"You mean that you'll help him, too, Lavelle?"

"Just that," said Lavelle firmly. "As far as Daley is personally concerned, I'm not interested; but we've got to remember that he's got a wife. Things like this hurt a woman, boys. Whether he's guilty or not, we've got to try and save him. He owes me a lot of money, which I never expect to collect. He got sore because I would not lend him another ten thousand."

"Then he needed money, eh?" queried one of the men.

"I suppose I shouldn't have mentioned that," said Lavelle. "He must have needed it, or he wouldn't have tried to borrow. Yes, he claimed that some one had stolen all his cattle."

"They did," said Uncle Jimmy. "Bud won't lie."

"All right," laughed Lavelle. "Let's have a drink."

CHAPTER VI

Cleve Lavelle thought he could well afford to be philanthropic. To his way of thinking, Bud Daley was the same as convicted, but Lavelle was willing to spend a few dollars in Bud's behalf, if only to make it appear that he held no animosity toward him. It would serve to put Lavelle in a good light with everybody.

The following day he rode out to the Triangle-D ranch. He half expected to find others out there, but was agreeably disappointed to find May alone.

"I had to come out to see you," he told her lamely, as they stood together on the ranch-house porch. "It was quite a shock to all of us to know that Bud had been arrested."

"I – I suppose every one is against him," she faltered.

"Not at all, May. Jim Miller and I are going to hire a good attorney for Bud."

"Are you? Oh, that is good of you both.

57

But, Cleve, do you think he did it?"

"That is hard to say. It looks rather tough for Bud, but you never can tell what a jury will do. We must face the fact that Bud has been acting wild, May. Character witnesses will have to testify, and all that.

"May, I know it is going to be an ordeal for you. But you won't have to testify. Just leave everything to us, and remember that I am waiting for you, little woman."

She shook her head sadly. "Not now, Cleve. I must help Bud all I can in this."

"Do you believe he is guilty, May?"

"Oh, I don't know," wearily. "He refused to tell the sheriff where he had spent the night, and he acted so queer – so utterly downhearted."

"I think I understand, May. That silver rosette was evidence against him, I understand."

"Yes, it belonged to Bud. The sheriff showed it to him. And a man was killed – shot?"

"George Findlay. May, we'll be lucky to get Bud a life sentence. They will try him for first degree murder, you know."

"First degree murder? Oh, Cleve, I didn't think of that!"

"Yes, it is true. Perhaps we can get him a sentence. Anyway, we will do the best we can,

May. He will have a preliminary hearing to-morrow. But, listen, May: when it is all over, we will go away and forget it all.

"No one will ever know where we have gone and we will start life all over again. I have enough money to keep us in luxury for a long, long time. Oh, I know how you feel about Bud.

"But we will not desert him. We'll do everything we can for the boy. But after it is all over, we will slip out of this country – just the two of us, May. No one can censure you for this."

But May Daley shook her head sadly. "It is awful good of you, Cleve. I want you to know that I appreciate everything you are doing for us. Perhaps I am just a little old fashioned, but – as long as Bud lives I will never marry again."

"You don't mean that, May?"

"Oh, yes, I do, Cleve."

"As long as he lives?" Lavelle frowned heavily. "Suppose he is sent up for life, May?"

"While there is life there is hope, Cleve." She tried to smile up at him.

"Oh, yes, I suppose there is, May. But why stick to a sinking ship? You can't wait a lifetime, little woman. I don't think that Bud would want you to do that."

59

"I know it looks foolish, Cleve. But, somehow, I've got just a little faith left, don't you see."

"But if Bud is sent up for life, won't it destroy your faith, May?"

"No."

Lavelle shook his head. "It is beyond me, May. But I suppose we will have to do the best we can."

"Thank you, Cleve. And it might be better if you do not come out here alone again."

"I suppose so," he agreed grudgingly. "But it don't seem right for you to be out here alone. Here comes Jim Miller."

They waited for the old man to ride up and dismount.

"I got hold of that lawyer, Lavelle," he said, after shaking hands with Mrs. Daley. "He comes high, but we've got to have the best."

"Sure thing, Miller. I just rode out to tell Mrs. Daley not to worry about anything."

"Well, yuh can't stop a woman from worryin', Lavelle. And she's got plenty of reasons for it."

"I suppose you're right, Miller. Well, I'll be going. See you all later."

They watched him ride away. Uncle Jimmy squinted sideways at Mrs. Daley, a quizzical expression on his face.

"He told yuh about us hirin' a lawyer, didn't he, May?"

"Yes, Uncle Jimmy. It is wonderful of you to do this for us."

"Yeah, I s'pose it was," dryly. "But I'd do more than that for you and Bud. What kinda gets me is why did Lavelle horn in and offer to pay half. Bud owes him a lot of money, and they ain't friends, May.

"Bud sure hates Cleve Lavelle. Personally I ain't got a bit of use for Lavelle – and he knows it. But he's slick – Lavelle is. He's educated and – crooked."

"But he's doing a wonderful thing for Bud, Uncle Jimmy. It takes a big man to do a service to a man he does not like."

"Yea-a-ah, I reckon it does, May. I had a dog once that wagged its tail and took a chunk out of my leg at the same time. Since then I've kinda kept my eye on tail-waggers. I sure don't like a friendly enemy."

"But I have heard men say that Cleve Lavelle was honest."

"Mm-m-m-m, well, I s'pose he's as honest as can be expected. Yuh can't draw that line too fine on a gambler. Honesty is a queer thing, May. It ain't human nature to be honest all the time."

"I think you could be, Uncle Jimmy."

"Like hell I could! Mebbe I'm honest with

my friends, but I'm not fool enough to carry it too far. Don't trust anybody. On the dollar it says, 'In God We Trust,' and that's about as far as anybody ought to trust. But you keep up yore nerve.

"Why don't yuh come over and live with us while this is goin' on, May? Ma Miller will be tickled to death to have yuh. As far as that's concerned, we'd all give three cheers. Can't yuh do it?"

"Thank you, Uncle Jimmy, but I think not – anyway, not just now."

"Well, you know it's yore home any time yuh want it. Ma will prob'ly be whoopin' over here right away. She ain't like me, Ma ain't. You'll sure have to tell her why yuh won't come. Well, take care of yourself, May. If yuh need anythin' or anybody – jist yelp once."

Cleve Lavelle was very thoughtful during his ride back to Modoc. Things were not coming as good as he had anticipated. He was madly in love with May Daley, and there was nothing he would not do to possess her.

"That was a real *faux pas* I pulled when I offered to pay half of a lawyer's fee to defend Bud Daley," he told himself. "She won't marry me as long as Bud lives, and I'm spending good money to keep him from the gallows."

He stabled his horse in Modoc, and met the sheriff on the street.

"How is the prisoner feeling?" asked Lavelle.

"I ain't felt on him lately," growled the sheriff. "Darned fool won't say a word; jist sets there and stares at the floor. I told him you was goin' to help hire the lawyer to defend him, and he told me to tell you to go to hell with yore lawyer."

Lavelle laughed and shook his head. "I imagine that Bud is going to be hard to save."

"Hard? Say, that blasted fool acts like he wanted a rope around his neck. He thinks I'm doin' this for spite – the danged fool! Sody an' Dinah swore they'd plumb ruin me if I didn't turn him loose."

Lavelle laughed. "They're joshing you, sheriff. Just forget the damage they did to my place. That is all in the game."

"All right. Yuh can't do anythin' with a pair of wild cats like them. I hope Bud Daley can get cleared, but I don't look for it."

"Do you think a Modoc jury will hang him, Breed?"

"No, I don't."

"Life sentence?"

"No, Lavelle, you've got to prove premeditated murder to get the life sentence, or the rope. That killin' was only a part of the hold-

63

up. He never went there with the intention of killin' anybody. He probably shot to save his own skin, and there ain't a jury in this country that would call it first degree murder."

"About twenty years, eh?"

"Somethin' like that."

"I suppose that's right," sighed Lavelle. "Well, we'll have to hope for the best, Breed."

But Lavelle's idea of the "best" did not coincide with what the sheriff meant when he nodded in agreement.

CHAPTER VII

The smoking-car creaked and groaned as the train swung slowly around one of the many sharp curves in the Modoc country. From the engine came the shrill whistle, sounding eerie and far away; from the wheels came the *clickety-click, clickety-click,* caused by the rail joints.

There were only two men in the smoker – "Hashknife" Hartley and "Sleepy" Stevens. Hashknife sprawled his six-feet-plus in solid comfort, hunched down so low that his coat hiked up around his ears and the lower part

of his lean face was hidden inside the unbut-
toned collar.

Sleepy was also at ease, although he did not
have as much length to distribute. His booted
feet were heel-hooked against the cushion of
the opposite seat, his nose slightly flattened
against the window as he stared out into the
darkness.

Both men were dressed in range fashion.
On the seat in front of them rested a couple
of cheap telescope valises, not at all bulged.
In fact, the sides were just a trifle sunken,
which would indicate that these two sons of
the range were travelling light.

Hashknife's right hand fumbled in the
pocket of his faded vest and drew out a
conglomeration of matches, cigarette papers,
a revolver cartridge and a piece of string. He
selected a paper, carefully replaced the other
impedimenta and glanced sidewise at Sleepy.

"Gimme yore Durham."

Sleepy's nose squeaked on the glass, as he
turned his head.

"Why don'tcha buy yuh some Durham
once in a while?"

Hashknife looked with disapproval upon
his partner.

"You ain't refusin' me yore Durham, are
yuh, cowboy?"

Sleepy grunted complainingly, dug into

a hip-pocket, and drew out a sack of the required brand.

"Yo're always stingy," observed Hashknife, helping himself from the inverted sack, and spilling a goodly quantity into the wrinkles of his shirt. "I always give you tobacco, don't I? Answer me that, why don't yuh? Any old time I have tobacco –"

"Any old time yuh do!" snorted Sleepy, accepting the sack and shoving it deep in his pocket.

Hashknife scratched a match and settled down to solid comfort again. Sleepy humped over, searching under the seat for a much-thumbed time-table, which he perused diligently for a while.

"The damn fool that got up this here time-table must 'a' knowed what he meant; but I don't," he declared. "It says here for yuh to read up. Read up, hell! It ain't no ways –"

"He means for yuh to read up the page," informed Hashknife.

"Didja think I thought he meant for me to read up the side of my boot? I know what he meant."

"Didja? When do we hit Modoc?"

Sleepy perused the page again.

"Up or down?" he asked.

"Which way are we goin'?"

"That's why I complains," explained

Sleepy, throwing the offending folder on the floor. "Nobody knows, except the *hombre* that wrote it – and he prob'ly didn't want to go to Modoc."

"Probably not," agreed Hashknife. "I'll betcha that Modoc don't care what he thought, though."

"I s'pose not." Thus Sleepy wearily. "Mebbe Bud Daley won't be a darn bit glad to see us."

"Yeah, he will," said Hashknife. "Old Bud's a good feller."

"Was," corrected Sleepy. "You ain't heard from him lately."

"Year ago last Christmas."

"And this is September. Danged near two years."

"That's right. Time sure does gallop along."

"And it wasn't nothin' but a Christmas card he sent yuh."

"That's all," Hashknife yawned widely and threw away his cigarette. "But it said he'd like to have us stop and see him some time, Sleepy – him and May."

"He had to be polite," grinned Sleepy. "I wonder if May is as pretty as she used to be? My golly, she sure was a dinger."

"Wouldn't change much in two years, or so. Yessir, she sure was pretty, Sleepy. I've seen a lot of girls, but I'll betcha that May Daley is the prettiest. She was too pretty to be safe and sound."

"M-m-m-m. I s'pose that Bud and her are gettin' along like old married folks. He probably puts on his slippers at night, don't play no poker, has to sneak a drink and then eat cloves. Smokes a pipe out in the woodshed and never says —, except when he refers to a irrigation project.

"How did he ever happen to go to this Modoc country, Hashknife? Didn't her folks live up here, or how was it?"

"I dunno about her folks, Sleepy. Bud met the owner of a cow-ranch up here and he offers Bud a good job, I reckon. That's the way it was told to me. Bud never said how it comes. Anyway, it don't make me no never mind. As long as we're passin' Modoc, I thought we might as well stop off to see him."

"Sure; I'd like to see old Bud. He used to be a forked sort of a puncher. Didja ever hear anythin' about this Modoc range?"

Hashknife shook his head.

"Nope. It's a big range, I reckon. There's a lot of cows shipped out of here. Remember them two painted broncs that Red Ellers had at Skyline. They was branded with the Bow-Knot. Red called 'em the 'Necktie' broncs. Them two was from Modoc. Red spoke

68

about the range once in a while, but I don't remember much of his talk."

They were silent for quite a while as the train lurched along through the hills. Then:

"Hashknife, I wonder if me and you will ever settle down?"

"I dunno." Hashknife smiled softly and rubbed his chin against the collar of his shirt. "I s'pose, so, Sleepy. I'm gettin' kinda tired of rammin' around the country, hornin' into other folks' business. Sometimes I wish I had a home, cowboy."

"Mebbe we'll hit a good range some day; a range where we'll want to settle down and take life easy. The years roll along, Sleepy. A buckin' bronc kinda makes me weary, and I'm gettin' slow with a gun. We're bound to slow up, don'tcha know it? We try to kid ourselves into thinkin' that we're just as fast as we was a few years ago, but age sneaks along and takes the snap out of us. Pretty soon me and you will buck up agin' a tough deal and we'll find that we're jist a fraction of a second slow."

Sleepy looked at Hashknife and laughed.

"All right, Methusalem; yo're about ready for the bone-yard."

Hashknife grinned and stretched in a wide yawn.

"All right. Anyway, I'm growin' timid
69

in my old age. Here comes the brakeman, lightin' his way with a lantern that don't give no light."

The brakeman came up the swaying aisle, grasping the backs of the seats, and when almost to the two men, he opened his mouth and yelled,–

"Moo-odoc!"

Hashknife and Sleepy uncoupled quickly and grasped their valises. Came a long-drawn wail from the locomotive, and the *clickety-clicks* sounded at longer intervals, as the brake-shoes gripped softly on to the wheels and slowly brought the train to a stop.

Hashknife and Sleepy were half-way to the doorway when the train stopped, with Hashknife in the lead. Suddenly he stopped and Sleepy bumped into him. For a moment Hashknife held firm, then turned quickly and shoved Sleepy out of the aisle and into a seat.

It was all done so quickly that Sleepy had no time to protest, and found himself sitting down, with Hashknife beside him, while through the doorway came two men. Sleepy blinked. One of the men was Bud Daley, the man they were going to stop at Modoc to see, and he was linked by a handcuff to the other man.

Then the train started on. The two men sat down a few seats ahead and across the aisle from Hashknife and Sleepy, without paying any attention to them. The two cowboys looked at each other, as if seeking an answer to the question that was uppermost in their minds. Bud Daley had not seen them. Just now he sat on the inside, looking straight ahead, saying nothing.

The other man turned his head and looked at Hashknife and Sleepy. He was a man of about forty years of age, hard-faced, keen of eye, and rather cruel of mouth. He merely glanced at them and turned back.

"Whatcha know about that?" whispered Sleepy.

"Bud has done had the deadwood put upon him, it seems."

The train gained speed again. It was evident that there were many curvings of the railroad on this side of Modoc, as the old coach protested against the contractions; while the engineer shrilled an almost constant warning.

They were possibly two miles out of Modoc when the train seemed to shudder its whole length as the brakes were applied heavily. The windows rattled and the doors banged loudly, while the whistle shrilled in short blasts. Then the train ground to a lurching stop.

The man to whom Daley was linked leaned across and peered out of the window. Sleepy flattened his face against the window and tried

71

to see something, but there was nothing but the dark.

"Prob'ly hit a cow," said Hashknife. "They sure can flag a train. I remember –"

Hashknife stopped and turned his head. Some one was coming down the aisle from the rear of the train. And that some one was two masked men, very business-like with their six-shooters.

"Don't move, gents!"

The one in the lead spoke sharply. Bud Daley jerked around, as did the man with him.

"Just take things easy," he cautioned. "That's what we're aimin' to do."

He walked past Hashknife and Sleepy, past Daley and the other man and turned, while his companion stayed farther back, guarding from the rear.

The man at the front took off his hat, disclosing the fact that the mask covered his entire head.

"Now," he said, "we will take up the collection. Just ante what you've got and don't hold out on the handsome gent. Remember that the man behind yuh is lookin' on, and don't start nothin'."

He held out his hat, and for the first time he seemed to notice that the two men were linked together.

72

"Well, well!" he exclaimed. "What have we here, folks? This must be the sheriff, takin' a prisoner to the big corral. Bet there ain't enough money on the two of yuh to buy a breakfast for a hummin' bird. Huh!

"Probably against the law, but I'm goin' to ask the officer to turn his man loose. Officer, have yuh got the key for that padlock?"

The officer squinted closely at him and was about to shake his head, when the bandit continued:

"Go ahead and lie, if yuh want to; you'll have to produce the key, just the same."

"All right," grunted the officer, taking the key from his pocket. "You've got the drop."

He snapped the handcuff loose. The bandit motioned for Bud Daley to get up, which he lost no time in doing.

"Beat it," said the bandit. "I've done all I can for yuh."

Swiftly Daley went to the door and swung off into the darkness. The bandit laughed, stepped past the officer and faced Hashknife and Sleepy, holding out his hat.

"Pardner," grinned Hashknife, "you've sure picked a blank. We've got what's left of a pair of tickets, an appetite, and nowhere in particular to go."

"Yeah?" The bandit glanced sidewise at the officer, who was sitting rigidly in his seat.

"Broke, eh?" he asked.

"Bent all to thunder," nodded Hashknife.

Swiftly the bandit reached into his pocket and drew out a handful of silver, which he tossed to Hashknife.

"Breakfast stake, gents," he laughed. "Sit just like yuh are and everybody will have a pleasant evenin'."

"Much obliged," said Hashknife, "and we're holdin' firm."

Swiftly the two bandits backed out of the car, shutting the door behind them. Then the officer sprang to his feet, drew a gun and ran toward the rear door; but there was no sign of the two bandits.

He came back cursing his luck, and went to the front door. From outside, farther up the train, came a fusillade of shots. The officer stepped out on the platform, but did not leave the car.

"What do yuh make of it, Hashknife?" queried Sleepy.

"I dunno, cowboy. Let's investigate."

They found the officer on the steps, leaning out, looking toward the front of the train. There was nothing to be seen. Then a man came running back, carrying a lantern. It was the brakeman.

"They're gone!" he yelled, as he came up to them. "Robbed every car, cut loose the express car and engine and took 'em away. Did they come into this car?"

"By golly, they sure did!" snorted the officer. "They took my prisoner away from me."

"Uh-huh," nodded the brakeman, too excited to even care who the prisoner might be. "They've done a good job of it, I guess. I've got to flag the rear, or some darned freight will come along and ruin us."

He trotted away up the track, his lantern bobbing in the dark.

"Got any idea who pulled the job?" asked Hashknife.

"No!" The officer was sore.

"You're the sheriff, ain't yuh?"

"Yeah."

"Waitin' for 'em to come back?"

"Waitin' for who to come back?"

"The hold-up men," said Hashknife innocently.

The sheriff grunted an unprintable word and dropped off the platform.

"Now yuh went and made him sore," complained Sleepy. "And he'll go away and leave us here alone. You don't show no judgment a-tall, Hashknife."

The sheriff heard it, but did not turn his head. The conductor came on to the platform and flashed his lantern into them.

75

"Did they collect back here, too?" he asked.

"They had it in mind," grinned Hashknife. "But it wasn't in the cards. What did they do – swipe the express car?"

"They sure did," said the conductor. "There must have been a bunch of 'em, because they worked all the cars at the same time. Some of the bunch took the engine and express car, but the rest of them had their horses handy and pulled out as soon as they had cleaned out the train. It sure was a neat job."

"Yeah, they knowed how to do it," said Hashknife. "How far are we from Modoc?"

"About two miles." The conductor swung his lantern outward.

"Who is that out there?" he asked.

"That's the sheriff," explained Hashknife. "He's lookin' for 'em to come back."

The sheriff turned and climbed back on to the platform, where he glared at Hashknife and turned to the conductor.

"I got on with a prisoner – a murderer," he said coldly, "and that gang turned him loose."

"Got on at Modoc?" asked the conductor.

"Yeah."

From down the track came the whistle of a locomotive. The conductor swung down and ran toward the front of the train, as the engine came backing around the curve, shoving the express car. There was a great bobbing about of lanterns near the car, as the train jerked from the jar of the coupling. Came a shrill blast of a whistle, and the train began slowly backing toward Modoc.

The sheriff turned and went back into the car, followed by Hashknife and Sleepy.

"Did you say that yore prisoner was a murderer?" asked Hashknife.

"What's it to yuh?" Thus the sheriff, sarcastic in his anger.

"Don't antagonise him, I tell yuh," warned Sleepy. "He's the sheriff, and he's got a awful mad spell upon himself."

"You think you're smart, don't yuh?" queried the sheriff.

"Well, mebbe I ain't so smart," said Sleepy seriously, "but I'm sure cautious. As far back as we've ever traced our family tree, there has been a cautious streak. Yessir, the old sap jist fairly oozes caution. Now –"

"Aw, to hell with your family tree!" snorted the sheriff.

"That's what I always told pa. I don't hold with no –"

"My gawd!" breathed the sheriff wearily, and moved away down the car.

Hashknife and Sleepy exchanged mirthful

77

glances and secured their valises. The train was backing into the depot at Modoc; so they swung on to the platform and headed up the main street of the town. Neither of them cared to stay there at the depot and hear a rehearsal of the hold-up; and it would likely be a relief for the sheriff to know that he was rid of their presence.

The main street of Modoc was not well enough lighted for them to get much of an idea of the town, but from the number of hitch-racks and the general appearance of the street it appeared to be a well-patronised cow town.

Most of the buildings were of the false-fronted variety, but here and there a two-story frame building lifted its top a trifle above the ordinary. It seemed that the business district was composed mostly of saloons.

Out in front of one, which bore the title of Rest Ye All, a fat cowboy was doing his little best to brace up the front of the place, while he sang mournfully:

"I don' wanna play in yore yard,
I don' like you any mo-o-o-o-ore.
You'll be sor-r-ree when you see me-e-e-e-e
Slidin' dow-w-wn our cel-lur-r doo-o-o-or.
You can't hol-ler dow-w-wn our rain bar'l,
You can't climb our apple tree-e-e-e;

You can't play in ow-w-wer yar-r-r-rd,
'Cause you won't be good to me-e-e-e."

Hashknife and Sleepy waited until he had finished and was still panting from clinging quaveringly to the personal pronoun at the end of the chorus.

"You've got a good voice, pardner," said Hashknife.

"Y'betcha," agreed the cowpuncher heartily. "Yuh like to hear me sing?"

"Nope. You've got a good voice – but not for singin'. Do yuh think this saloon would fall down if yuh moved away?"

The cowpuncher grunted, shoved himself away from the wall and grasped a porch post firmly with both arms.

"Now whatcha goin' to do?" asked Sleepy.

"Sing. I'm sad, don'tcha know it? My gawd, but I'm sad. And when I'm sad – I seeng, thasall."

"Oh, yo're a seenger, are yuh?" laughed Hashknife. "Well, hop to it, brother. Far be it from us to curtail yore sadness."

"That's real kind of yuh, I'm sure."

The cowboy almost fell off the sidewalk in trying to bow his appreciation, but Sleepy steadied him and helped him get a fresh grip on the post.

Hashknife and Sleepy passed on into the
79

saloon, while the puncher lifted his voice in a wailing sort of dirge, which bore a certain resemblance to "When You and I Were Young, Maggie."

The Rest Ye All was rather a pretentious place inside. A long, mahogany bar extended down the left side, backed by an ornate but damaged mirror. The walls were decorated with oil paintings of considerable merit, mounted in gaudy frames. Even the lamps were decorative.

The bar-room proper was about thirty feet long by twenty feet wide, with an archway at the rear which led to the gambling parlour. As Hashknife and Sleepy stopped at the bar they caught a glimpse of several gaudily dressed women in the rear room, and to their ears came the rattle of poker-chips, the whir of a roulettewheel, the soft voice of a dealer at a stud table.

The pink-faced bartender, with a diamond horseshoe in his shirt front, lifted his eyebrows in interrogation. Hashknife and Sleepy made known their wants and drank silently.

"Yuh got quite a place, here, pardner," observed Hashknife.

"Yeap." The bartender carefully polished the bar and replaced the bottle.

"Swellest place this side of New York."

"Coverin' a lot of territory, ain't yuh?" asked Sleepy.

"I've never been to New York," grinned the bartender.

"You spent much time between here and there?" queried Hashknife.

"Nope. I've been as far East as Cheyenne."

"Thasso? You must like to travel."

At this time the fat cowboy came inside and weaved up to the bar, where he goggled at Hashknife.

"I'm Sody Slavin," he announced, and added, "and I'm sad within me. They took m' friend Bud Daley t' prison, don'tcha know it? And all he done was t' kill a cashier and steal twenty thousand dollars. This here country is gettin' too antisheptic for me, by gosh."

Hashknife squinted at Sleepy, who was making faces at himself in the back bar mirror. Came the sound of excited voices outside, and the sheriff came in, followed by several men. Sody squinted at the sheriff and reached for him with both hands.

"Whazzamatter?" blurted Sody. "Where's Bud?"

"Aw, go to hell!" snorted the sheriff, shoving Sody aside, and heading for the back room.

Hashknife and Sleepy followed them into the gambling room. Cleve Lavelle was just

81

coming in from the rear, and the sheriff went straight to him with the news, blurting it loud enough for every one to hear.

Those at the games quit playing and crowded around, while the sheriff told them what had taken place. But he only told of the cutting loose of the express car and the loss of his prisoner.

"They robbed the passengers, too, didn't they?" asked Hashknife.

The crowd turned their attention to Hashknife. Breed squinted at him and shook his head.

"No. That brakeman got so excited that he thought everybody was robbed. None of the passengers were molested, except me."

"How much did they get?" queried a cowboy.

"Not much," said the sheriff. "They dynamited the express safe, but didn't get much. The messenger said that it was empty."

"And Bud Daley got away from yuh, eh?" chuckled another.

"Oh, hurray! Hurray!" whooped Sody, who had followed them in. "Hurray f'r ol' Bud."

Sody's enthusiasm drew a laugh from the crowd and lessened any sympathy that might have gone to the sheriff.

82

"It seems to me that there ought to be more action and less talk," observed Hashknife. "A train robbery and an escaped murderer ought to make a sheriff do somethin' besides talk himself tired."

Dug Breed squinted at Hashknife and Sleepy closely.

"Takin' quite a lot of interest in this, ain't yuh?" asked Breed sarcastically.

"Well," Hashknife grinned softly, "I'm a citizen, and I kinda like t' feel that I'm protected by the law."

"You ain't," declared Sody, seriously. "P'tect yourself, stranger. The law means right, but she's plumb flat-footed around here."

Breed grunted angrily and looked around, as though wondering just what reply to make. Hashknife grinned at Sody, who nodded owlishly and essayed a few jig-steps.

"Who are these two men, Dug?" asked Lavelle.

"Hanged if I know!" snapped Breed. "They were on the train."

"We're just a couple of helpless mortals," said Hashknife slowly. "We're lookin' for a peaceful place, thasall. We finds that we ain't safe on a train; so we unloads here. Ain't no objection to it, is there?"

"Not that I know of," said Lavelle.

"Well, that's nice of yuh, I'm sure," said Hashknife. "We both thank yuh. My pardner is kinda timid; so I does the talkin'."

"Myah!" snorted Breed angrily, and turned his back on Hashknife.

"Goin' to git up a posse, Dug?" asked a cowboy.

"Y'betcha." Breed turned and walked swiftly back toward the bar-room.

"Let's go and find a hotel, Sleepy," said Hashknife.

"Hotel, hell!" snorted Sody. "Git yore broncs and come out to the ranch with me."

"We ain't got no broncs, Sody," grinned Hashknife.

"Ain'tcha?" Sody took this under advisement. "I'll git yuh some."

"Not to-night," said Hashknife. "We'll hit the hay in a hotel to-night."

"All right," grudgingly. "I'll see yuh 'morrow. Yo're the kinda folks I like, and you'll like ol' Jim Miller's outfit. He's got the JM outfit; *sabe?*"

They talked outside and Sody pointed out the hotel down the street.

"Who's the feller that the sheriff talked to back there in the saloon?" asked Sleepy.

"Tha's Cleve Lavelle."

"Outside of his name, what is he?"

"Mos'ly everythin'," said Sody. "Owns

84

everythin', almost. Owns the 76-A ranch, too."

"Was Bud Daley a friend of yours?" asked Hashknife.

"Yo're damn right. Bud's a dinger. And he's loose, ain't he? Tha's fine, y'betcha. Good ol' Bud. I don't like Dug Breed. He's the sheriff. I'm jist as pop'lar with him as a set of delirium tremens."

"And they put the deadwood on Bud, did they?"

"Oh, pos'tively. Twelve good men and true said he was guilty. Uncle Jimmy Miller and Cleve Lavelle hired the bes' lawyers yuh ever seen, but they cinched him. Bud wouldn't talk. My Lord, I can't con-shee-ve of anybody not talkin', in a case like that. I'd talk so much and so fast that the judge would never have a chance to pronounsh shentence. That's me – a man of many words."

"The sheriff was takin' him to the pen, wasn't he?"

"Exactly. Oh, indeed, he was, yessir. Bud was shentenced yesterday. They gave him twenty years."

"Who do yuh reckon took him away from the sheriff?" asked Hashknife.

"Who? I dunno. I've got to do a lot of thinkin' before I can shay pos'tively. I'll buy a drink."

"Not to-night," laughed Hashknife. "Do you think they'll catch Bud Daley?"

"I refuse to state." Sody grew very wise and serious. "If Bud don't want to be caught, tha's another matter en-tirely. Bud's forked, don'tcha know it? He'll fight. Yessir, I kinda look for gore to be spilled before they git ol' Bud agin.'"

They shook hands with Sody and went on toward the hotel.

"What do yuh think of it, Hashknife?" queried Sleepy.

"Looks like Bud Daley has growed horns and a tail, Sleepy. But yuh never can tell. We'll sleep over it."

"We ought to have stayed on that train," said Sleepy. "The first thing we know we'll be sharpenin' our horns agin' – and this don't look like a one-man proposition."

CHAPTER VIII

Sody Slavin was too elated over Bud's escape to remain inactive; so he hunted up Dinah, who was also full of bottled cheer, and told Dinah that they were going out to Bud's ranch to break the news to Mrs. Daley.

"Gug-gug-gug –" gurgled Dinah.

"Sure, it's good," assured Sody. "Where's yore horse?"

"Ca-ca-ca-ca –"

"Came in the cart, eh? F'r gosh sake! Well, I ain't in jist the right shape to ride a horse m'self. Let's go and git one more drink and then we'll ride out there."

They went back to the Rest Ye All saloon and drank to a successful voyage in the cart. But they did not stop at one drink.

In the meantime Cleve Lavelle had talked with the sheriff about Bud's escape, and found that the sheriff did not believe Bud would go home. But Lavelle was curious. He saddled a horse and rode out of town, just ahead of Sody and Dinah.

The sheriff had hinted that he did not think that Bud would stay in the Modoc country and take chances on being caught. It seemed sensible enough except that Bud was a daredevil sort of person and might have some ideas of his own.

Lavelle knew that Mrs. Daley refused to go out to the JM ranch, and was living alone at the Triangle-D, although he had not seen her alone since the night of Bud's arrest. Lavelle had been an interested spectator all during the trial, and had been called as a character witness for the State.

He had tried hard to temper his answers, but the prosecuting attorney happened to know about Lavelle's dealings with Bud Daley, and the witness could only tell the truth. There was no denying the fact that Bud needed money.

Sody Slavin's testimony showed that Bud had been too drunk to have done the deed, but the prosecution seemed to prove that Sody Slavin was too drunk that evening to even make an estimate as to Bud's condition. So Sody's testimony did not help.

Every one had wondered why Bud would not testify in his own defence. Lavelle had tried to figure out just why Bud took so little interest in the case. Mrs. Daley did not take the stand, nor did she and Bud exchange a word during the long trial.

To every one it seemed that Bud welcomed a sentence. Uncle Jimmy was right when he claimed that no Modoc jury would convict Bud of first degree murder, and no one was surprised when the judge sentenced him to a term of twenty years.

Lavelle had tried to converse with Bud during the trial and afterwards, but Bud refused to talk.

Lavelle thought of all these things as he rode out to the Triangle-D that night, and he wondered if it was possible that Bud knew he had tried to take May away from him. He did not think such a thing possible, because of the fact that Bud had not mentioned it.

Lavelle knew that Bud was hot-headed, and it never occurred to him that Bud might not kill a man for trying to break up his family affairs. So he decided that it must be something else.

He rode up to the Triangle-D ranch-house and dismounted at the porch. The house was in darkness, and Lavelle hesitated quite a while before knocking. He was just a trifle nervous, for fear that Bud might have come home.

He knocked several times before he heard Mrs. Daley's voice.

"Who is it?" she asked.

"Cleve Lavelle," he answered.

She came closer to the door. "What are you doing here at this time of night?" she asked.

"I had some news for you, May. Bud escaped from the sheriff to-night, and I thought you might want to hear about it."

"Bud escaped? Thank God! Cleve, you're not joking, are you?"

"No, it is no joke, May. No one knows which way he went."

"But how in the world did he escape?"

"It's quite a story, May. If you are not dressed, put on some clothes and let me tell

89

it to you. I hate to talk through a door."

"Well," she said dubiously. "All right. It won't take me long."

She went back to her room at the rear of the ranch-house and began dressing, while Lavelle leaned against a porch-post and lighted a cigar. He was highly elated to think he was going to have a chance to talk with May – and with no chance of an interruption.

He smoked thoughtfully, wondering why it took a woman so long to get dressed. Suddenly he heard a sound. It came from far down the road – the rattle of wheels, a burst of raucous laughter.

Lavelle knew that the road ended at the Triangle-D, and this equipage must stop there; so he did the only thing possible under the circumstances; mounted his horse hurriedly and rode back into the hills.

Sody and Dinah were having a terrible time with their horse and cart. The horse was a buckskin three-year-old, which Dinah was breaking to harness, and this was its second lesson. In fact this was its first time in harness alone – and the harness was none too good, a makeshift job by Dinah, who was not a harness maker.

"This horsh ain't got no shensh," declared Sody thickly. "Got plenty of road, but the darn fool inshists on goin' where there ain't no road. Gimme them lines, Dinah! My gosh, who ever tol' you you could drive? You ain't drivin' – yo're herdin' the poor thing. Now, wash me closely, cowboy."

Wham! He hit the animal across the rump with the end of the lines, and the frightened horse fairly leaped from between the shafts, almost throwing Dinah out of the cart. In fact it left him leaning so far back that there was little chance of him regaining his balance.

Dinah was really too inebriated to attempt speech. Sody saw at a glance that his companion was about to leave the equipage; so he made shift to assist him back. And while the cart bounced and bounded like a rubber ball over a cobbled street, Sody managed to haul Dinah back to safety.

"Stay with me, cowboy!" he yelped. "I'm for yuh, as long as yuh keep yore mouth shut. Whoo-ee."

The "Whoo-ee!" was what Cleve Lavelle had heard. It was the old cowboy yell of triumph.

But Sody's triumph did not last. He slapped Dinah on the back, yelled defiance at the moon – and discovered that he had lost both of his lines. The buckskin horse was running like a mad thing, and the cart was only on the ground at intervals.

91

He yelled in Dinah's ear, "Thish is jus' goin' t' be too bad! I've lost my lines!"

"Dud-dud-don't nun-nun –!"

"The heck I don't need 'em! Git ready to rise and shine, old timer! The Triangle-D ain't far away, and the road ends!"

Dimly the situation dawned upon Dinah, but it was all right as far as he was concerned. Straight ahead bulked the little ranch-house, and the horse was heading straight for it.

Sody thought of leaving the cart ahead of the crash, but his limbs refused to function; so he opened his mouth and began singing, –

"Oh, bury me not on the lone prairee-e-e-e-e!"

Crash, one wheel of the cart collided with a corner of the porch, just as Mrs. Daley opened the door, and Dinah went right in past her, turning a complete cart-wheel and falling full length on his back.

The sudden shock was almost too much for her. Instead of a quiet word with Cleve Lavelle, a cowboy had come flying past her and was now lying in the middle of the room, making funny noises as he tried to pump air back into his empty lungs.

She had heard and felt the crash of the cart striking the porch, but did not connect it with a runaway. In fact, it all happened so suddenly that she hardly knew what to think.

She stepped quickly to the door and looked out, but all was serene. As she looked back Dinah sat up, goggling owlishly at her. She recognised him now. It seemed so much like a nightmare that she pinched herself to see if she was really awake.

Dinah's eyes were wide with astonishment. Possibly he had forgotten where they were going. He took a deep breath.

"Dud-dud-dead and in huh-huh-heaven!" he blurted.

"Dinah Blewette!" she gasped. "What on earth brought you here at this time of night?"

Dinah did not seem to know exactly. He stared at her wonderingly. Perhaps the whisky had been partly driven from his brain. Finally he bobbed his head slowly.

"Huh-huh-how d-d-d-do!"

"Don't try t' talk!" snorted a voice at the door, and Mrs. Daley turned to see Sody Slavin, with the brim of his hat around his neck and one sleeve of his shirt missing. Otherwise he seemed in good shape, except that his face wore a dazed expression.

"Sody Slavin!" exclaimed Mrs. Daley. "What does this all mean?"

"Well'm," Sody swallowed painfully. "Yuh shee, the horsh didn't see the housh," Sody shifted painfully. "I sheen it comin', ma'am, but I couldn't dodge it."

93

"Runaway?" she asked.

"Oh, my, yesh! Bigges' yuh ever shaw. Whim! Wham! Bang!" Sody almost fell down in trying to pantomime the accident.

"And it threw Dinah right through the door!" marvelled Mrs. Daley.

"Thasso? Huh!" Sody scratched his head. "I thought he got tired of my comp'ny. Git up, Dinah! I'm sure s'prised at yuh for sittin' down in the presence of a lady."

"What on earth were you doing out this way at this time of night?" she queried.

Sody rubbed his nose thoughtfully. What was it he came to tell her? Oh, yes, he remembered now.

"It was about Bud," he said solemnly. "Yuh shee, Bud got loose t'night, Misses Daley. The sheriff was takin' him on the train, and shomebody held up the train, shee? And they stuck a gun in Dug Breed's face and made him let Bud loosh. And nobody knows where Bud is. My, my! The sheriff is shore."

"Somebody held up the train?" wondered Mrs. Daley. "Why, that is queer, Sody. And took Bud away from the sheriff?"

"Jus' like takin' candy from a baby, thasall."

She came closer and peered into Sody's face.

"Sody, did you have anything to do with it?"

"Me? Gosh A'mighty, woman – no! Wish I had. I'm jus' as mystified as you are. I – I'm prob'ly more mystified than anybody in the world. Dinah, are you gonna git up?"

Dinah got up and clung weakly to a chair.

"But they won't be after Bud again?" asked Mrs. Daley anxiously.

"Y'betcha – sure. But he's loost now. We jus' came out to tell yuh the good news, thasall. I dunno how we'll git back. That cart is awful for to look upon, but the horsh is tied to the corral fence."

"Ri-ri-ri –" began Dinah quaveringly.

"That's right, we'll ride 'm. We'll ride 'm double, eh?"

Mrs. Daley laughed softly, and wondered where Cleve Lavelle went. Somehow she was glad these two drunken cowboys had driven him away. "Perhaps," she thought, "he is out there in the hills, waiting for these two men to leave."

"Well, I s'pose we might as well pull out," said Sody.

"I was just wondering if you boys wouldn't like some good coffee," said Mrs. Daley.

"Coffee?" Sody grinned delightedly. "I sure would."

"And some doughnuts?"

"Gee cripes! Shay, I'm glad we stopped, Dinah. Mrs. Daley, would it be too much trouble for yuh not to tell anybody 'bout us havin' run away? Yuh shee, I was drivin'."

"I wouldn't mention it for the world, Sody."

"Now, tha's sure fine of yuh, ma'am. Bow to her, Dinah."

Dinah bowed solemnly, and Mrs. Daley proceeded to build a fire in the kitchen stove. She was glad they would stay and have coffee, because she felt sure that Lavelle would tire of waiting for them to leave, and go back to Modoc.

She was right in her surmise. Lavelle did not wait long. He was too far away to know who was with her, but decided that it was some one from town, possibly Jim Miller, who had ridden out to tell her the news. So he silently circled the ranch and went back to Modoc, cursing his ill luck, while Sody and Dinah tilted back in their chairs and watched Mrs. Daley cook a big pot of coffee.

CHAPTER IX

There was little excitement in Modoc the next morning. The sheriff and his posse, which consisted of Charley Morse, the Deputy sheriff, "Monte" Sells, foreman of the 76-A ranch, Frank Asher, of the same outfit, and Steve Harris, of the 4X, had not come back to town.

Hashknife and Sleepy ate breakfast late and ran into Sody Slavin at the post office. Uncle Jimmy had come in with him, and Sody lost no time in introducing Hashknife and Sleepy to him.

"Sody tells me that you was on the train last night when it was held up," said Uncle Jimmy.

"Yeah, we were there," grinned Hashknife. "Yuh see, we were on our way here to make Bud Daley a little visit. We came in by stage through the Brant River country to Dixon; and found ourselves so close to Modoc that we figured it would be kinda handy to drop off and see Bud."

"Thasso? You knowed Bud before, eh?"

"Sure. We used to work with him. Tell us somethin' about the trial, will yuh?"

97

Uncle Jimmy related everything, according to the evidence, while the four of them sat on the edge of the board sidewalk and dug their heels into the dirt.

"There wasn't a lot of evidence ag'in him," explained Uncle Jimmy. "That rosette off his chaps looked bad to the jury. Bud wouldn't tell where he was that night, and everybody knowed that Bud needed money. He jist sat there and let 'em convict him, without even arguin' about it.

"Me and Cleve Lavelle hired lawyers for him, but they didn't help Bud much, 'cause Bud wouldn't talk. He jist didn't seem to give a damn what they done to him. Old Jordan has been doin' his dangdest to find out what Bud done with that money, but Bud won't never tell.

"If he lives to serve that twenty years, he'll have twenty thousand dollars. Mebbe he looks at it thataway, I dunno. Didja ever know his wife, Hartley?"

"Yeah. Knowed her before she married Bud. This must 'a' been danged tough for her."

Uncle Jimmy nodded sadly.

"Shucks, yes. May is the salt of the earth."

"They can't take the ranch away from her, can they?" asked Hashknife.

"I dunno. Anyway, it ain't worth enough to battle about."

"Bud wasn't a success as a cattleman, eh?"

"He was doin' all right until somebody stole all his cows."

Hashknife's eyes opened a trifle wider and he looked sidewise at the old cattleman.

"Stole all his cows?"

"That's what Bud says. He had a nice herd started. Bought out the old Triangle outfit, about three miles west of here, and had it registered as the Triangle-D. Bud had a little money, but not enough; so he borrows five thousand from Lavelle, who owns the Rest Ye All over across the street.

"Bud always was a gambler; so he takes that borrowed money and tackles the roulette. He sure was right that day, and he annexes ten thousand from Lavelle. That gives him fifteen thousand, and he soaks it all into cows."

"Was Lavelle sore?" asked Hashknife.

"No. Lavelle is a gambler. Bud should 'a' paid back that money right then, but he didn't. The round-up was about three weeks ago, and there ain't a Triangle-D animal in the Modoc range.

"I don't *sabe* it no more than anybody else does. A lot of 'em think that Bud picked 'em up quietly and shoved the herd through the

Crooked Cañon country and over to Black Wells."

"To keep from payin' Lavelle that five thousand eh?" queried Hashknife.

"Seems to be the idea," nodded Uncle Jimmy. "He even went and tried to borrow ten thousand more from Lavelle, but didn't git it."

Hashknife laughed softly and shook his head.

"Our friend Bud has become a salty sort of a gent, it seems."

"Could he drive his cows out of the country and not have it known?" asked Sleepy.

"Could be done," said Sody. "Bud's place is kinda away by itself, and right on the old trail to Black Wells. He could 'a' worked easy like, bunched 'em in the hills back of his place and hammered 'em out at night, and it wouldn't take more than a few hours to put 'em well into the Crooked Cañon country."

"But," demurred Hashknife, "if he sold 'em in Black Wells, it ought to be easy to find out."

Uncle Jimmy spat viciously and shook his head.

"The only thing yuh ever find out in Black Wells is that it's a darn good place to keep yore mouth shut."

"It's a good place to dispose of stock,"

100

grinned Sody. "They don't even look at brands."

"Lavelle and Bud were good friends?"

"Well," grinned Uncle Jimmy, "he loaned Bud five thousand dollars, and then he paid half of his lawyer bill. I reckon that's friendship, ain't it?"

"Kinda has the ear marks," smiled Hashknife. "Who do yuh reckon held up the train and turned Bud loose?"

"More friendship," laughed Sody. "Ol' Bud was pop'lar."

"Bud didn't trail with train robbers, did he?" asked Hashknife.

Uncle Jimmy squinted closely at Hashknife and placed a horny hand on Hashknife's knee.

"You ain't pious, are yuh, Hartley?" he asked slowly.

Hashknife laughed and shook his head.

"Then don't build yuh any glass houses and start throwin' rocks. Friendship is friendship, accordin' to my way of lookin' at it, Hartley. I've heard that there was a heck of a lot of bad folks in the Modoc country – but there ain't none of us that say a prayer before we go to bed, 'cause we ain't afraid of anybody shootin' us in our sleep."

"I beg yore pardon, Jim Miller," said Hashknife softly. "I reckon I understand how it is."

"Thasall right," nodded Uncle Jimmy. "You know how we stand now."

"I'd like to see Mrs. Daley," said Hashknife. "Yuh see, we came here to see Bud, and we'd like to do what we can for his wife."

"Mebbe we can get horses at the livery stable," suggested Sleepy.

"Yuh can, but yuh won't need to," grinned Sody. "I dragged in a couple of extra broncs with me this mornin', and they're over at the hitch-rack, waitin' for yuh."

"You fellers kinda hypnotised Sody, didn't yuh?" laughed Uncle Jimmy. "He wouldn't do that much for me. I remember —"

"No, yuh don't," interrupted Sody. "I've done a lot for you."

Uncle Jimmy got to his feet and brushed off his knees.

"There ain't no use arguin' with yuh, Sody," he declared. "You ain't noways changeable. I never did see anybody as set in their ways as you are. I sure made a awful mistake when I made you foreman of the JM outfit — I should 'a' given it to yuh."

"It ain't too late," grinned Sody. "But if yuh do I'll fire yuh right off the reel. I'd want capable men on my ranch."

They went over to the hitch-rack and untied the horses. Sody had brought a

102

couple of hammer-headed, evil-eyed animals for Hashknife and Sleepy; but he was not trying to play any tricks on them.

"They'll likely buck a little," he told them. "Mebbe they'll buck more than a little, but I didn't want to insult yuh by bringin' a couple of rockin' chairs for yuh."

"If we get ditched it'll be all yore fault," laughed Hashknife as he swung aboard.

Neither animal made any effort to buck, and Sody nodded wisely.

"Yuh can't fool a bronc," he declared as they rode out of town. "Them animals knowed right away that it wasn't no use tryin' to shuck you two fellers; so they don't waste their energy."

"I reckon we'll find Ma out at Bud's place," said Uncle Jimmy. "She didn't say she was goin' out there, but she will."

"Y'betcha," nodded Sody. "Where there's sufferin', you'll find Ma Miller."

It did not take them long to ride the three miles to the Triangle-D ranch-house. A sorrel buggy team was tied to the fence near the house, and near the front porch was grouped a number of saddled horses.

"That's Ma's buggy team," observed Sody, "and them broncs belong to the sheriff's posse. I c'n tell Dug Breed's black animal."

They rode up and dismounted, just as
103

Breed and his posse came out of the front door. Breed squinted hard at them, but did not say anything. Ma Miller, a tall, raw-boned woman, followed them out.

Her jaw was set at a belligerent angle, and it was plain to be seen that she was not at all in accord with the officers. She ignored Uncle Jimmy and the rest and centred her indignation upon Dug Breed and his men.

"Git off the ranch – the whole caboodle of yuh!" she ordered in a masculine voice. "Dug Breed, you ain't got the feelin's of a coyote. Trompin' in like that! Didja expect to find Bud Daley here? You can't keep a man when yuh do git one.

"Anyway, you're a sweet lookin' gang to be enforcin' the law. Yeah, I mean it, too. Monte Sells and Frank Asher! Steve Harris! Say, when did you snake hunters git a licence to hunt criminals? If we had a sheriff that'd uphold the law, you fellers would be huntin' the high places yourself."

They were riding away, making faces at each other, and Ma turned belligerently toward Uncle Jimmy and the others.

"You sure can tell 'em things, Ma," laughed Sody. "Whooee! Meet Mister Hartley and Mister Stevens, Ma. Gents, this is Ma Miller. Most men has a better half, but Uncle Jimmy has a better seven-eighths."

Ma grinned and shook hands with them.

"Ma, I'm sure glad to meet yuh," laughed Hashknife. "Yo're worth a lot to a man whose eyes hankers for the home folks."

"That's a reg'lar speech," laughed Ma Miller. "Didja say yore name was Hartley?"

"Yes'm. Hashknife to m' friends."

Mrs. Daley had come to the door and was staring at Hashknife. Her face was tear-streaked and her eyes shadowed with sorrow, but she held out both hands at the sight of Hashknife.

"I heard your name," she said gladly. "Oh, I'm so glad to see you, Hashknife. And there is Sleepy Stevens!"

Hashknife took both of her hands, while Sleepy crowded in to shake hands with her.

"How in the world did you ever happen to come here?" she asked.

"We came here to visit yuh, Mrs. Daley."

"When did you come?"

"We was on the train that Bud was on, and we seen him turned loose."

Mrs. Daley looked away, her lips trembling.

"Then you know what has happened to us, Hashknife?"

"Y'betcha. We've heard a lot of the story."

"Haven't you heard all of it?"

Hashknife shook his head slowly.

"Nobody knows all of it, ma'am. Yuh see, the last chapter ain't been written yet."

"By gosh, there's a lot of sense in that, too!" exclaimed Ma Miller. "May has been grievin' her heart out; but she don't know yet how it's goin' to turn out."

May smiled wistfully and shook her head.

"I don't see how things can be better for us, Ma."

"Well, they ain't got Bud in no danged prison," reminded Sody. "He's got a fightin' chance."

"Quit talkin' about it," grunted Uncle Jimmy.

"Anyway, I am awful glad to see you two boys," smiled Mrs. Daley. "Bud speaks about you so often."

She turned to Ma Miller and took her by the hand.

"Ma, you'll like these two men. Bud swears by both of them. He says that Hashknife Hartley — no, I won't repeat it — but it used to make me jealous. He used to wonder what old Hashknife and Sleepy are doing to-day, and wish that they would come along and advise him on certain things."

"I told yuh they were reg'lar folks," Sody

grinned at Uncle Jimmy triumphantly. "By golly, I can pick 'em – drunk or sober."

"Are you going to stay a while?" asked Mrs. Daley.

"Yuh never can tell about us," smiled Hashknife. "We ain't gentlemen of leisure, but it kinda seems that we don't stay put in one place very long."

"You don't look like a pair of drifters," observed Ma Miller.

"No, ma'am," Hashknife shook his head. "We travel under our own power."

"Bud used to say that they were the best cowpunchers in the world, but they never punch cows," said Mrs. Daley. "He said they were always too busy to work."

"What did he mean by that?" asked Sody.

Hashknife laughed and began a cigarette.

"Yuh see, we're kinda unlucky – me and Sleepy. Everywhere we go we find somebody in a jam. We jist can't mind our own business – somehow. Personally, I'd like to settle down and grow old with the country; but Sleepy can't git over his childish ways; so I reckon we'll keep – movin' along."

"You won't have much for yore old age, will yuh?" asked Uncle Jimmy.

"Yeah, we'll have quite a lot," smiled Hashknife. "It won't be anythin' that yuh can cash in at a bank. And when we die, we won't leave nothin' spendable. There ain't nobody dependin' on either one of us, except the other."

"I think I know what you mean," said Mrs. Daley softly. "Bud told me some of the things you have done."

"Likely magnified 'em," grunted Sleepy. "Bud always did have a big imagination. We've been lucky, thasall."

"I hope it will never change," said Ma Miller earnestly.

"It won't, Ma – as long as we're right," said Hashknife. "Sometimes it's hard to be right. Humanity is a queer thing. We might do wrong through friendship, through a wrong hunch, or believin' a lie."

"If yuh want jobs, I'll give 'em to yuh," stated Uncle Jimmy. "I ain't got a danged thing for yuh to do, but that ain't goin' to interest nobody but me. Mebbe it'll be worth it to have somebody for Sody to argue with. He'll leave me alone. Harry McKee won't argue with him, and Dinah Blewette stutters so bad that he ain't got a chance in the world; so Sody makes me miserable. If there's anythin' on earth that I hate, it's an argument."

"Yeah, you do," growled Sody. "You hate it like yuh hate fried chicken. When you won't argue – you're in danged bad shape."

108

"Thasso!" Uncle Jimmy bristled belligerently. "Lemme tell yuh somethin', you –"

"Jim Miller, don't start it!" snapped Ma Miller. "My gosh, you two gallinippers make me tired. Your arguments never have no beginnin' nor end. And, anyway, this ain't no time nor place for arguments."

"He started it, Ma," protested Uncle Jimmy. "He always starts 'em, if yuh notice. All I done was to offer these two men jobs."

"They never asked yuh for a job, Jim."

"Didn't they? I s'pose I've got to be asked, have I? Say, who owns the JM ranch? Ain't I got a right to offer a job without bein' asked?"

"I'm the foreman," reminded Sody.

"Are yuh?" Uncle Jimmy teetered on the balls of his feet and hooked his thumbs over his cartridge belt. "You are, are yuh? That makes you quite important, eh? Anybody'd think you was the Grand Exalted Ruler of the Universe, Sody. I made yuh foreman, didn't I? Anybody'd think you was born thataway? You sure do wear yore honours lightly, fat feller. Well, go ahead and hire 'em, why don'tcha?"

Sody turned and looked seriously at Hashknife and Sleepy.

"Did you fellers want a job on the JM ranch?" he asked.

Hashknife and Sleepy both shook their

heads. Ma Miller threw back her head and laughed, and even Mrs. Daley forgot her troubles long enough to join in the merriment.

"That was a lot of talk wasted," said Ma Miller, wiping her eyes with her apron. "But that's like Jim and Sody. I've been tryin' to convince May that she ought to come over to the JM ranch and stay with us a while. She can't stay here alone."

"By golly, she sure can have the JM if she wants it," said Uncle Jimmy. "That's her home. You come and live with us, May. Ma needs somebody to argue with, don'tcha know it. Then she'd leave me alone. I sure don't git much peace in this world – and yuh never can tell about the hereafter."

Hashknife laughed and threw away his cigarette.

"Now, that's a good idea," he said seriously. "Suppose Mrs. Daley goes up to yore ranch and leaves us in charge here. We've got to have a place to sleep, and I don't like that hotel. We'll run the ranch for a few days."

"Why, you wouldn't want to do that," protested Mrs. Daley.

"Sure, we'd enjoy it," said Sleepy enthusiastically. "We hate hotels."

"But there's nothing here to do."

"*Esto buena*, as the Mexican says," laughed Hashknife. "If we wanted work, we'd 'a' grabbed Uncle Jimmy's offer."

"Well," said Mrs. Daley dubiously. "I don't know. There isn't a very big stock of food in the house, and the –"

"Ne' mind the food," grinned Sleepy. "We'll haul some out. If we see a fat JM on the hill, we'll eat steaks."

"I'll herd one down to yuh," offered Uncle Jimmy. "Or yuh might beef a 76-A. Lavelle wouldn't miss one."

Hashknife happened to be looking at Mrs. Daley and noticed the quick flush that came to her white cheeks at the mention of Lavelle.

"Lavelle owns the 76-A?" asked Hashknife.

"Yeah," nodded Uncle Jimmy. "He's the he-hawk of this country. Two of his men are in that sheriff's posse, but I'll betcha he'll give 'em hell when he finds it out."

"Mr. Lavelle has been very kind to us," murmured Mrs. Daley.

"Well, I'm glad we've got a place to stay," observed Hashknife, looking round. "Yuh don't mind if we keep them two broncs for a while, do yuh, Uncle Jimmy?"

"I should say not. Keep 'em as long as yuh want 'em. If there's anythin' else on the JM that yuh want, come a-hootin' and have at it. Ma, you and May git yore stuff into the

111

buggy. By golly, it's goin' to be fine to have May back home ag'in. If Bud –"

Uncle Jimmy stopped and squinted toward the hills. The tears had come to Mrs. Daley's eyes again, but she turned and went into the house, while Ma Miller glared at Uncle Jimmy before following her inside.

It did not take them long to pack up what clothing Mrs. Daley wanted to take to the JM ranch, and they drove away down the dusty road. Uncle Jimmy and Sody shook hands with Hashknife and Sleepy, promising to drop in on them very soon.

"Bring yuh down a fat yearlin' t'morrow," promised Uncle Jimmy, "and mebbe Sody'll bring yuh a hatful of aigs."

They went out through the rear gate and swung into the hills, cutting across to the JM, which was about three miles to the north. Hashknife and Sleepy locked the house, mounted their horses and headed back toward town, itemising the groceries they would need.

"Bacon," said Sleepy. "What do yuh think of the proposition?"

"May's prettier than she ever was," said Hashknife thoughtfully. "We gotta have a few cans of tomatoes."

"Ma's a dinger, Hashknife. How about some beans?"

"Beans? Sure. Who do yuh reckon stole Bud's cows? And matches. I never did live in a place where there was enough matches. And Uncle Jimmy ain't no – Sleepy, don't let me forget canned peaches. I love peaches. How's yore Durham?"

"Mine's all right; how's yours? You ought to buy some tobacco for yourself, Hashknife. Honest, yuh ought to do that. And if you forget bakin'-powder, I'll massacree yuh. 'Member the time we – Say, that posse sure got told about themselves, didn't they? Ma sure rattled their skeletons for 'em."

"And salt'n pepper," added Hashknife. "I suppose that posse went back to Modoc and got drunk."

And so they enumerated jerkily all the way back to Modoc, filled with joy at the prospect of doing their own cooking and of eating it.

To one who did not know Hashknife Hartley they might have classed him with the average irresponsible cowboy, but back in his serious mind was the germ of an idea.

Sleepy did not originate ideas. He was content to follow Hashknife's lead in all things; content to sit back and let the lanky one work out the salvation of both. In many things Sleepy Stevens was a pessimist, an arguer, but open to conviction. He was outspoken in his likes and dislikes, as was

Hashknife, ready to do battle for a friend, caring little for the future. Men had said that these two were animated antidotes for range poison – a title which had caused them much amusement.

Neither of them was a wizard with a six-shooter. In fact, their marksmanship was criticised by both; but cold nerve had carried them through some tough battles against men who wère reputed to be lightning on the draw.

Both of them were good average rifle-shots, although neither would admit it. Sleepy loved trouble. His idea of bliss was to swap lead with somebody. Not hand to hand swapping; but a battle in the hills, long-range rifle work. The *sping-g-g* of a high-power bullet, ricocheting off the rocks, was music to his ears.

But Sleepy was not blood-thirsty. It was all in the day's work with both of them. And their work had made them confirmed fatalists; confirmed humorists. They had laughed at death, laughed at life.

"And why not?" Hashknife had questioned. "Nobody knows what life is. Neither do they know what death means. When yuh see somethin' that you don't know nor understand, ain't it better to laugh than to cry over it?"

Hashknife was partly right when he proph-
esied that the posse had gone back to Modoc
to get drunk. Breed and his deputy were cold
sober, but the others were having their fill at
the Rest Ye All bar, while their weary horses
nodded at the hitch-rack.

Hashknife and Sleepy tied their horses at a
rack in front of a general merchandise store
and were ordering their groceries, when Breed
came in. He watched them sack up their stuff
and then followed them outside.

"Goin' batchin'?" he asked.

Hashknife grinned and nodded, as he tied a
sack behind the cantle of his saddle.

"We're goin' to live at Bud Daley's ranch
for a while."

"Oh, thasso?" The sheriff was interested.
"You knew Bud, didn't yuh?"

"Yeah, we used to know him pretty
well."

"His wife goin' to stay there?"

"Nope. She's gone to the JM ranch. We'll
be there alone."

"What's the idea?"

Hashknife knotted a string and squinted at
it critically before he said: "Well, now I don't
reckon you could call it an idea, sheriff. We
jist got tired of the hotel, thasall."

"Uh-huh."

The sheriff scratched his chin thoughtfully.

Naturally he wanted all the information possible. Bud Daley was still at large, and this might be a scheme to get him a grub-stake. But it might not be an opportune time to mention such a thing, he realised; so he nodded and walked away.

Sleepy went to the hotel, paid their bill, took their valises and came back to the horses. The half broke bronchos objected to the valises, but were soon convinced that this excess baggage was there to stay. Dug Breed watched them ride away and grew thoughtful.

These two men rode well, he observed. They both wore guns, and their guns and belts seemed more practical than ornamental.

"That tall jasper ain't no man to fool with," he mused. "I dunno about the shorter one. I wish I knew what they are goin' to do out there at Bud's ranch. They're friends of Bud's, that's a cinch. But I can't stop 'em. There's no law against 'em living out there."

Breed shook his head, rubbed some of the dust out of his sleepy eyes and went across the street to the Rest Ye All.

CHAPTER X

"Yo're goin' to stay right here, May Daley," declared Ma Miller, as she showed May a room in the ranch-house. "Yuh can't help Bud none by stayin' down at that lonesome ranch-house.

"Too proud, are yuh? Huh! May, this ain't charity. Not by a darn sight. You'll earn yore board and room by just bein' around here. I need somebody to talk to, May. I've talked to men so much that I'm usin' more cuss words than Sody does, and that's a caution to cats.

"Uncle Jimmy was sayin' just the other day that I needed a refinin' influence around the house. Honest, I'm glad yuh came. Things must be gettin' pretty bad when an old pelican like Jim Miller gets to hankerin' for refinement."

"Oh, I think that Uncle Jimmy is a dear," laughed May.

"Dear! Huh! For gosh sake, don't let him hear it. If yuh ever say anythin' good about him, where he can hear it, my life ain't worth goin' ahead with. Jim's as vain as a peacock. Honest.

"We had a new school teacher a year or

117

so ago. Yuh know, Jim is on the school board. Anyway, he heard this teacher say that she liked Jim Miller because he was so delightfully eccentric.

"Jim got all swelled up over it and bragged like a darn fool to everybody, until Sody looked it up in the dictionary, and found that it meant 'cracked,' or somethin' just like it."

"Did he quit braggin' about it, Ma?"

"In front of Sody he did. But Jim's all right. Lordy, he's got a heart as big as an ox – and liver and lights in proportion, I reckon. Say, if you ain't got a night-shirt, yuh can wear one of mine. Red outin'-flannel. Ha, ha, ha, ha, ha! First time Jim seen me in one of 'em he rolled me up in an Injun blanket. Thought I was on fire."

May Daley laughed chokingly as Ma Miller pantomimed the rolling operation.

"And that wasn't the worst of it, May. Jim had to tell everybody about it, and about a week later we went to a dance in Modoc and I wore a red dress. I wondered why everybody laughed."

"Ma!" Uncle Jimmy called from the living-room. "When yuh get tired of runnin' down yore legal, lawful husband, I wish you'd start supper. Sody and Dinah are settin' on the front steps gnawin' at a post."

"Always hungry!" retorted Ma Miller.

"They ought to incorporate that in the weddin' ceremony – love, honour, obey, and cook. Mebbe a lot of us would baulk."

"I been wantin' to get a Chinaman, Ma," reminded Uncle Jimmy.

"Not while I live and can shuffle my feet, Jim Miller. I can believe in hydrophoby skunks, snow-snakes, and high-behinds, but nothin' can convince me that Chinamen can cook vittles fit for me or mine. Tell Sody to get me some wood."

"Hey, Sody! Ma wants wood!"

"I heard it all," said Sody sadly. "Why pick on to me? Why not name Dinah in the complaint?"

"Somebody has got to do it, Sody."

"Shore they have. I'll jist play one game of seven-up to see who gets it, Uncle Jimmy. C'mon, Dinah. Low man stuck, eh?"

The rocking-chair in the living-room creaked, and three sets of high-heeled boots went down the front steps, heading for the bunk-house.

"I'll have to get my own wood," said Ma Miller. "You just set down and take it easy, May."

Mrs. Daley followed her to the kitchen, and together they secured sufficient wood for cooking the meal.

"You can peel the spuds, if yuh want to,"

said Ma. "Jim or Sody usually does it, and sometimes I can get Dinah to uncover a few. But I've always got to nail 'em before they get a chance to gamble over it."

Ma Miller busied herself for several minutes. Then, –

"I s'pose yo're worryin' a lot about Bud, May. Don't blame yuh a bit. Wish we knew where he is. Darn him, I wish he'd come here to eat his meals."

"I – I wonder where he eats, Ma?" Anxiously. "And where he sleeps. Oh, it is awful to think of him out there in the hills, with no one to help him."

"And a sheriff lookin' for him all the time. But Dug Breed never caught anybody. May, I can't believe that Bud ever done that hold-up. I don't care a whoop what the jury said! Bud convicted himself, I tell yuh. Why, that danged gallinipper never even opened his head."

"Ma," Mrs. Daley looked at her tearfully over the pan of half-peeled potatoes, "Ma, why wouldn't he talk to me? He never even told me good-bye. The sheriff asked him if he wanted to tell his wife good-bye, and he – he said – no."

"That's right, honey." Ma Miller wiped away a tear, and slammed a pan on the stove to cover her emotion. "And, by golly, it wasn't as though it was an over-night trip, either. He might at least have said good-afternoon to yuh, May."

"Yes, he might – but he didn't, Ma."

"Well, I dunno. The longer I live, the less faith I have in humanity. If Jim Miller went away to be gone twenty years, and didn't tell me good-by – I'd fix him when he got back."

They looked at each other and laughed through their tears. Ma Miller went to May and patted her on the shoulder.

"Don't mind me, honey. The Lord gave me a queer tongue. Just you keep on smilin'. What do yuh know about Hartley and Stevens?"

"Oh, they are fine boys, Ma. Bud always swore that they were the best that ever lived. They were down in the Red Hill range country for a while, but they knew Bud before he came there. Hashknife Hartley, so Bud always said, sees things that the ordinary man never notices.

"There had been a lot of cattle rustling going on in the Red Hills, and Hashknife and Sleepy came there to investigate for the Cattle Association. It took them just a week to jail the guilty ones, and Hashknife's testimony sent them all to the penitentiary."

"Is that a fact? May, I wonder if they are trying to find out the truth of things around

121

here. They would help Bud, wouldn't they?"

"I – I'm sure they would, Ma."

"I'll betcha! May, I've got a hunch that somethin' is goin' to happen – somethin' good."

"I – I – I – I – I –" It was Dinah at the kitchen door.

"You lost, didja?" queried Ma.

Dinah nodded sadly. "Ye-ye-ye-ye –"

"Thasall right," said Ma. "The wood is all in and the spuds are bein' peeled, Dinah. No, don't try to thank me."

"Gug-gug-good!" exploded Dinah. "Th-they ch-ch-ch-ch –"

"Cheated yuh, eh? Yuh knew they would. Run along, cowboy."

"Isn't it too bad he has such an impediment in his speech," said May, after Dinah had gone away.

"Not so bad. His tongue will never get him into trouble."

CHAPTER XI

The 76-A ranch was located about five miles north-east of Modoc. Lavelle had spent much money in making it the finest cattle-ranch in the country, although he did not spend much of his time at the ranch-house. A Chinese cook and a Chinese house boy had charge of the ranch-house, while Monte Sells was in charge of the ranch.

While no one had objected openly, there were many who did not exactly care for Sells, "Red" Blair, Frank Asher, "Mesa" Caldwell, and Brent Allard, Lavelle's cowpunchers. They were a hard-riding, hard-drinking crew of men, who gave Lavelle back their salaries over the green cloth, or drank it up over his polished bar.

Just now Red Blair and Brent Allard were enjoying a cigarette *siesta* in the shade of a big cottonwood near the big red stable at the 76-A. Red was lying flat on his back, his sombrero half across his face. Blair was a big man, with high cheek-bones, eyes deeply set under bushy brows and a flaming thatch of red hair.

Allard was a smaller man, colourless, tow-headed, but with a cruel mouth and a deep knife scar along his right jaw-bone. His cigarette hung limply from his lips as he humped over on his haunches and drew meaningless patterns in the dirt with his forefinger.

"I'd jist like t' know where Monte got his information," he said musingly.

123

Red Blair grunted and brushed a fly off his nose.

"He won't tell," continued Allard complainingly.

"– the flies!" Red grunted angrily, and sat up slowly to reach for a match. "Wonder if the posse caught Bud Daley yet?"

Allard shook his head and spat disgustedly.

"I'd jist like to know who stuck up Dug Breed."

"You ought to buy a dictionary," said Red wearily.

"Why?"

"You want to know so damn much."

"Yeah?" Allard dug savagely at the dirt. "I don't like to risk my neck for nothin', Red."

"You didn't risk yore neck."

"Didn't, eh? Aw, I know. You fellers think yuh can do anythin' yuh want as long as yo're workin' for Cleve Lavelle. Sure. He makes the sheriff and all that, and we're perfectly safe. But Lavelle didn't have nothin' to do with this, yuh must remember."

"He'd have somethin' to say," replied Red easily. "Yuh don't see the sheriff moseyin' around here, do yuh? Dug Breed knows which side his bread is buttered on, y'betcha."

"Stick yore head in the sand like an ostrich," grunted Allard. "That bird ain't

124

the only animal that rams its head out of sight and thinks nobody can see the rest of it."

"Why don'tcha go back to Oklahoma?" queried Red. "You ain't got the guts of a canary bird, Allard."

Red got to his feet, slapped his hat on his head, and squinted toward the road.

"Here comes Monte and Frank," he grunted, "and they're ridin' kinda loose."

Allard got up and they walked down to the corral where Monte Sells and Frank Asher had dismounted. Both men had been drinking and were in a joyful mood.

"We've been upholdin' the law," declared Asher, yanking the saddle off his panting animal, and almost upsetting himself.

"Yuh look like you'd been holdin' up a saloon," observed Red caustically.

"Didja find Bud Daley?" asked Allard.

"Find hell!" snorted Monte angrily. "Breed led us all over the damn hills in the dark. Mebbe he thought Bud would be carryin' a lantern."

"Yeah, and we went to Bud's house," laughed Asher. "Breed wanted to search the place, didn't he, Monte? Ma Miller was there. And what she told Breed was aplenty. Man, she sure read his sign for him."

"Read our epitaph, too," laughed Monte.

"Said we'd be high-tailin' it a long time ago, if we had an honest sheriff."

"Wonder where Bud went," said Allard.

"You better go down and join Breed," snorted Monte. "He's in the same fix you are."

"Did Breed give up the posse idea?" asked Red.

"As far as we're concerned," laughed Monte. "Lavelle was sore as a boil when he found that me and Frank was on the posse. Lavelle spent a lot of money tryin' to clear Bud; and he said he'd be damned if he wanted his men to help run him down the hills."

"Bud's wife still at the ranch?" queried Red.

"She's gone out to the JM," said Asher. "Anyway, that's what Breed told us before we left. Couple of strange punchers goin' to batch at the Triangle-D. Friends of Jim Miller, I reckon. They came out there about the time that Ma Miller hoodled us out of the house."

"Who are the strange punchers?" asked Red. "Didn't you hear their names?"

"Aw, Breed said that one of 'em was named Hartley, or somethin' like that. I don't know whether that's the name or not."

· Allard moved in a little closer, his lower lip sagging as if his half-smoked cigarette weighed pounds.

"Didja say 'Hartley,' Frank?"

"It was somethin' like that, Brent. I didn't pay much attention to the name."

"What kind of a lookin' feller, Frank?"

"Tall, skinny geezer."

"The other one was shorter? Kinda sad-faced and bow-legged?"

"That's him."

Allard brushed the cigarette off his lips and cleared his throat.

"That's Hashknife Hartley and Sleepy Stevens, by gawd! And I'm draggin' m'self off this range right away."

Monte Sells stared at Allard for a moment and broke into a laugh. Allard was squinting into space, his lips shut tight.

"What's the matter with you, Allard?" asked Monte. "You act like this feller might be gunnin' for yuh."

Allard shook his head quickly.

"No, he ain't gunnin' for me, Monte. At least, I don't think he is. But he's jist bad luck, thasall. I've seen his work – him and the bow-legged one."

"Why, you darn fool!" exploded Red angrily. "What can he do to you?"

"Not a damn thing!" snapped Allard. " 'Cause I ain't goin' to give him a chance. I'm goin' away – a long ways away."

"Not a gut in his body," declared Red inelegantly, pointing at Brent Allard. "Runnin' away from a spook."

"Thasso?" Allard flushed indignantly. "I've got all I need to keep me in a healthy condition, Red. And I'm goin' to keep 'em too. I wonder what them two are doin' around here."

Monte laughed shortly and hitched up his belt.

"They're just livin' at the Triangle-D, thasall."

"No, that ain't all," declared Allard. "Jist livin' ain't all where they're concerned."

"They were on the train the night of the hold-up," volunteered Frank.

"Uh-huh-h-h," said Allard triumphantly. "And you – fools think they're jist livin' here, eh?"

"Detectives?" queried Red a trifle uneasily.

"Malignantly," nodded Allard. "Hashknife Hartley can read yore mind, I tell yuh."

Monte laughed sarcastically and slapped Allard on the back.

"We'll see that our minds are clear of all evil, when we meet him, Brent. Don't be a fool. Hartley is just a human bein', ain't he? Well, I reckon we know how to deal with human bein's, don't we?"

"You said a heap," laughed Red. "If that pelican monkeys around us, we'll sure clip his wings, eh, Monte?"

"Hop to it," said Allard wearily. "But don't ask me to help yuh. I've warned yuh, thasall."

Allard turned and walked toward the bunk-house, while the rest of the cowboys looked after him, a laugh on their lips.

"Scared plumb stiff," declared Monte.

"And," observed Frank seriously, "it ain't like Brent to get scared thataway. He ain't no coward, Monte."

"That's right," muttered Red. "Brent's no coward, but right now he's scared. Mebbe we better investigate this Hartley person. It's better to be safe than sorry, Monte."

"That's true enough, Red. If he's here to find trouble, we'll sure guide him to plenty of it, won't we?"

"Danged right. And we'll label it in big letters, so he won't make no mistake. I'm kinda anxious to see this pair of whip-poor-wills, m'self. If they're dangerous, the sooner we find it out the better it will be for all of us."

"Mebbe they'll be in town to-night,"

grinned Monte widely. "If they're not, we know where they will be."

"That's my idea, too," laughed Red.

CHAPTER XII

Dug Breed was greatly disgruntled over his failure to find any clue to Bud Daley's whereabouts. He had not expected to find any trace of the train robbers. The express messenger and the engine crew said that there were several masked men in the gang; but their failure to do more than damage the through-safe and the interior of the car hardly made them worth bothering with.

Breed was of the opinion that the hold-up was planned only as a means of taking Bud Daley from him, because of the fact that an organised gang would hardly stick up a train and blow the express safe unless they were reasonably certain of some remuneration.

But he could hardly understand just who would do such a job. The JM. outfit might have done such a thing. There were four men at that ranch. But Breed knew well that Sody Slavin was too drunk that night, and that

Uncle Jimmy Miller had been at the depot to see Bud leave. This was a perfect alibi for the JM.

"I don't *sabe* it a-tall," he told Charley Morse, his deputy, who was tilted back in an office chair, trying to coax a tune from a home-made banjo.

Charley balanced the banjo on his knee while he rolled a cigarette. Charley was not very keen mentally, and Breed's worries bothered him very little.

"Bud's prob'ly got a gun by this time," he observed.

"Yeah, he prob'ly has," agreed Breed.

"And he'll use it, too."

"What would you do if yuh had twenty years starin' yuh in the face? Wouldn't you use a gun, Charley?"

"Y'betcha."

"All of which makes Bud a dangerous man," mused Breed.

"Gotta outsmart him, thasall," declared Charley, picking up his banjo and hunching to a comfortable position.

"Yeah? How would you outsmart him, Charley?"

Charley yawned widely and rubbed his nose. Charley was not slighted when they passed around noses.

"He's got a wife, Dug," said Charley.

131

"He'll want to see her, won't he? Stick him up when he comes home."

"Uh-huh?" Breed squinted reflectively. It was not such a bad idea, at that, he agreed.

"He'll come home after grub, I reckon," added Charley. "Feller has got to eat."

"But his wife ain't home, Charley. She's at the JM ranch."

"Does Bud know it?"

Breed glared at Charley and spat disgustedly.

"How in hell do I know what Bud knows?"

"Have to watch both places, I reckon."

"All right. As soon as it gets dark we'll pull out. You go to the JM and I'll watch Bud's place. It ain't likely that he knows she went to the JM, Charley. Don't let nobody see yuh; *sabe*. Cache yourself away where yuh can watch the house all night."

"Hell!" Charley threw the banjo on the table and fumbled for a match. "Set there all night, eh? I had a hell of a good idea, didn't I?" Charley rubbed an ear violently. "Next time I'll keep my danged mouth shut. Bein' real smart didn't git me anythin'."

"You probably won't have much to do, Charley."

"Only keep awake. I played poker all night, I'd have yuh know."

"That ain't my fault. You better take
132

a shotgun along, 'cause you're cock-eyed already."

"Don't need no shotgun. What I need is sense enough to keep my mouth shut when I get a smart idea. What about them two strange cowpunchers out there at the Triangle-D? You get to monkeyin' around out there, Dug, and one of them grim-faced jiggers will prob'ly fill yuh with lead."

"They ain't got anythin' against me, Charley."

"Not yet," dryly. "You keep on monkeyin' – and they will have. Somebody tells me that they're old friends of Bud."

"They're runnin' his ranch for him."

"Livin' there, yuh mean, Dug. That tall jigger is *hyas cultus,* if yuh ask me." Charley knew enough of the Chinook jargon to use it at times.

"Meanin' that he's pretty bad, eh?"

"To monkey with," amended Charley. "His gun ain't no darn Christmas tree ornyment."

"Well, they can't bluff me," declared Breed. "If Bud Daley comes to the Triangle-D or to the JM ranches, we'll sure put the deadwood on to him. I'm dependin' on you to keep yore eyes peeled to-night."

"That's fine," yawned Charley. "Yo're puttin' yore trust in one of the best

133

deputy sheriffs that ever made a mistake and told the sheriff what to do. But to-night he ain't no owl, and about all he can hear is a bed callin' his name."

Breed went across the street to the Rest Ye All, where he sat in at a poker game. It was shortly before dark when the boys from the 76-A rode in and proceeded to regale themselves with plenty of liquor.

Breed noticed that they talked among themselves, ignoring the games, but drank plenty of whisky. Then they went out and were gone quite a while, drifting back in singles to meet at the bar again.

"Lookin' for somebody," Breed decided.

More cowboys drifted in, and in a little while Breed cashed in his chips and drew out of the game. Charley was at the office, with the two saddled horses, and in a few minutes they were out of Modoc and on their way, unseen by any one in the town.

About a mile out of town the road forked; one road leading to the JM and the other to Bud's ranch. Breed gave Charley final instructions and they separated.

There was no moon, but the sky was brilliant with stars. The road led along the slope of the hills, winding in and out of the hollows, crossing an old water-course, deep in the shadows of cotton-wood and willow, only to lead straight back into the sage-covered hill again.

Farther on it skirted the side of a hill, and Breed could see a light in the ranch-house window. Somewhere a horse nickered shrilly. Breed drew up, dropped to the ground and placed a hand over his horse's muzzle. After a minute or two he went on, walking and leading his horse.

The road led in past the stable, but Breed dismounted in the brush before reaching the stable, tied his horse and went cautiously past the corral and stopped at the corner of the stable. He was not in a position to watch the entire house; so he went back to an open window, climbed inside the stable, and felt his way to the door, which he found unlocked.

He shoved the door partly open and sat down. From here he could see part of the front porch, all of one side and the kitchen door. The horses moved uneasily for several moments, but settled down to their feeding.

He could not see the lighted window now. It was warm there in the barn. He found a saddle blanket and a box with which he made a comfortable seat, and settled down to his long vigil. He felt sure that Bud

135

would not show up before midnight, if at all.

Then he did the natural thing under the circumstances – fell asleep. After all, a sheriff is only human, and he was comfortable.

He did not know what awakened him, but he suddenly found himself wide awake and staring out through the doorway. A man was between him and the house, bulking large in the half-light. As far as Breed could determine, this man was watching the house. Then he began moving slowly toward the front porch, apparently cautious.

Breed grunted to himself, drew his gun, and stepped softly outside.

"He ain't takin' no chances," he observed to himself. "Bud always was cautious, and he don't know who might be in the house."

Swiftly but softly Breed crossed toward the man, who was so intent on the house that he did not think of any danger from the rear, and when within about twenty feet, Breed stopped and spoke:

"Put 'em up real high, young feller."

The man whirled swiftly, and his answer was an orange-coloured streak of fire and the crashing report of a revolver. Breed felt the wind from the bullet, ducked instinctively and shot from his hip. The man grunted, staggered sideways and went to his knees, shooting as fast as he could, while Breed's gun stabbed streaks of fire in his direction.

Then a bullet struck in the gravel a few feet from Breed and threw a spray of fine rocks into his face. He ducked sideways and almost ran into a bullet which was coming from another direction; while from three different directions came the barking reports of six-shooters, all throwing lead at the sheriff.

Breed did not stop to question any one. He almost decided not to bother with a horse, but his course was in that direction. Luckily the corral gate was open, which gave him a chance for a long run before his jump, and he barely scraped a heel on the top pole of that seven-foot corral.

Hashknife and Sleepy were in bed when the first shot caused them to sit up like a pair of mechanical toys. The next shot sent them out of bed, gun in hand and running toward the door; but the fusillade caused Hashknife, who was in the lead, to stop short, and Sleepy bumped violently into him.

"What the hell are yuh tryin' to do – knock m' teeth out?" demanded Sleepy. "Yore danged elbow is jist like a bay'net."

"Aw, hire a hall!" snapped Hashknife. "What's goin' on around here, anyway?"

The firing ceased. Some one ran past the front porch, crunching heavily on the gravel. Hashknife cautiously opened the door and peered out. All was serene. From far away came the sound of a running horse, and somewhere in the hills a coyote barked snappily and wailed dismally, as if protesting against being disturbed.

"Well, now that sure does beat heck by a neck!" exclaimed Hashknife. "Jist why do they pick our little ranch to stage a battle?"

"Some of it was danged close, too," said Sleepy. "Them first few shots were right up against our house."

Hashknife led the way back to the bedroom, where they proceeded to dress and buckle on their belts.

"She's a small world," complained Sleepy, "when they have to come out to our yard to have their fights. What do you make of it, Hashknife?"

"Mebbe somebody was havin' fun with us, Sleepy."

"Well, they've had it, cowboy. I'm a-quiverin' all over."

They went out on the front porch and looked around. There was not a sound to be heard. Hashknife led the way around the corner and stopped short. A man was lying flat on his back, looking up at the sky, arms outstretched. A few feet from him was a heavy six-shooter.

Hashknife knelt beside him and felt of his heart. He was still breathing, and as Hashknife touched him he groaned aloud.

"He ain't dead, is he?" asked Sleepy.

"Yeah. They always groan thataway after they're dead."

Hashknife got to his feet and dusted off his knees.

"Grab his feet, Sleepy; we'll take him in the house."

They carried him in and placed him on the floor, after which they lighted a lamp and looked him over. It was Red Blair; but he was unknown to them. Hashknife made a brief examination of him and pronounced him a case for the doctor.

"And we ain't got no time to lose," declared Hashknife. "There's a buckboard down at the stable, and I reckon them other two horses are broke to harness. We'll take this jasper to Modoc and find out who he is."

It did not take them long to harness the team, load the wounded man into the buckboard, and head for town. The road was not very smooth, but Sleepy held the man down, while Hashknife drove the team at a stiff gallop most of the way.

And Dug Breed did not stand on ceremony. He had made a flying leap for his horse, and the echo of the shots had hardly died away when Dug Breed was travelling toward Modoc as fast as his horse would carry him, and Dug Breed always rode a fast horse.

He swore wonderingly as soon as he could catch his breath. He did not have the slightest idea what it was all about. If that was Bud Daley, who was doing all the shooting at him, he wondered.

"He was sneakin' up on the house," he told himself. "Doggone it, that's what he was doin'! I hit him, I know that much. My Gawd, there was lead flyin' from all directions. I'd sure like to know what it was all about, but that wasn't no time for me to set around and ask questions."

He did not slacken speed, until he began to wonder what he was running away from; then he stopped. For several minutes he debated on the advisability of going back. There were plenty of reasons why he should, but he decided against it.

"Whoever I shot is either dead or crippled," he told himself. "And they can't keep it a secret."

As he started to ride on a horseman came

140

down the road toward him. The sheriff drew swiftly aside and let the rider pass him before accosting him.

"Is that you, Charley?" he asked.

The deputy whirled in his saddle and jerked upon his reins.

"Well, for gosh sake, what are you doin' here, Dug?" he asked.

"I'd like to know the same about you."

"Thasso? Well, I'll tell yuh right now that I'll be darned if I'm goin' to set out there in the dark."

"Thought you'd sneak back and crawl into bed, eh?"

"I wasn't sneakin', Dug. I just thought if you was darn fool enough to do it, I was willin' to let yuh go ahead and – but what are you doin' here? I thought you was goin' to watch the Triangle-D ranch-house."

"I did," said Breed, as they rode on toward town. He told Charley Morse what had taken place at the Triangle-D ranch, and the deputy whistled wonderingly.

"Yuh don't know who yuh killed, Dug?"

"I dunno whether I killed anybody or not."

"And yuh didn't wait to see who shot at yuh?"

"I did not."

"Huh! Reckon it was Bud Daley?"

"I thought it was."

141

"Uh-huh. Prob'ly was. And when yuh busted into him, them other two punchers started pastin' lead at yuh. Too bad I wasn't with yuh."

"Yeah, it is." Dryly. "Prob'ly one or both of us would have got killed."

"Prob'ly. What are yuh goin' to do about it, Dug?"

"Wait and see what happens, Charley. I don't reckon they knew who I was; so it's an even break. By keepin' still, mebbe we'll find out all about it."

CHAPTER XIII

It was past midnight when they drove up to the Rest Ye All. The place was fairly well filled, and Lavelle was at the bar, talking with several men, when Hashknife asked the bartender where he could find a doctor.

"Somebody hurt?" asked Lavelle.

"Yeah," replied Hashknife, "I dunno who he is. There was a lot of shootin' goin' on out at Daley's ranch, and this feller must 'a' got in the way of some lead. He's out there in the buckboard."

There was a general exodus to the front of

the saloon, and Hashknife soon found out who the man was. Lavelle took immediate charge and sent a man for the doctor.

"Mind telling me how it happened?" asked Lavelle.

Hashknife told him what he knew of the matter, but it was evident that Lavelle did not believe a word of it. Some one was sent after the sheriff, who appeared in a few minutes. He made a great show of asking questions, which no one could answer – except the sheriff himself – and he grew absent-minded, trying to appear at ease and to puzzle out what Red Blair was doing at the Triangle-D ranch, and who did the shooting after Red Blair went down.

He felt sure that Hashknife and Sleepy were telling the truth, as strange as it might seem to those who did not know. The doctor took charge of the wounded man, and Hashknife and Sleepy went back to the ranch, wondering what Lavelle's cowpuncher was doing at their doorstep, and who shot him.

"This," declared Hashknife, "sure as hell has got me fightin' my head, Sleepy. What did that red-headed puncher want out there? Who shot him? Was all them shots fired at the jasper that shot this Red Blair? Who were they? Sleepy, I'll be darned if this ain't some mix-up."

"Do yuh reckon Bud Daley was mixed up in it?" queried Sleepy.

"That's hard to tell, Sleepy. There's a lot of things to work out. F'r instance, who stole Bud's cows? Who robbed the bank? Who held up that train? Why did they take Bud away from the sheriff? What in hell was Red Blair doin' out there to-night, and who shot him? My gosh, no wonder Sherlock Holmes was a hop-head."

"Well," laughed Sleepy, "yo're happy, ain't yuh, cowboy?"

"Gittin' thataway," laughed Hashknife.

They unsaddled at the stable and went to the house, but drew all the curtains before lighting the lamp. Hashknife started toward the bedroom, but stopped and squinted toward a corner of the living-room.

"Sleepy," he asked, "wasn't there a rifle in that corner when we left here?"

"By golly, I think there was, Hashknife. It was there the last I seen of it."

"Uh-huh," Hashknife strode into the kitchen with the lamp and looked around, with a wide grin on his face.

"We've had a visitor," he stated. "Bud's been here after a gun and a grub-stake, Sleepy. That dog-gone pantry is jist about cleaned out, and I'll betcha we're shy a horse and saddle."

144

"That's fine!" grunted Sleepy. "Takes a load off m' mind. I was kinda worryin' about Bud, but we know he's all right now."

They went back to the bedroom and undressed.

"I wish we'd 'a' been here," said Hashknife thoughtfully. "I've got a lot of questions to ask that danged fool."

"What about, Hashknife?"

"Oh, about hang-nails, and if he's bothered with dandruff," replied Hashknife sarcastically. "If I've got to live with an idiot, I might as well be crazy, too. Good-night."

Being the employer of Red Blair, Lavelle was naturally interested in the shooting. As soon as Hashknife and Sleepy had gone away, Lavelle had his horse saddled and rode to the 76-A, where he found every one in bed and the place in darkness.

He hammered on the door with the butt of his quirt, loud enough to wake every sleeper on the ranch, but there was no immediate response.

"Wake up, you sleeping beauties!" he yelled.

"Oh, it's you, eh?" It was Monte Sells, who stepped from the corner of the house, gun in hand, while from the opposite corner came

Brent Allard, similarly armed.

"Heard yore knock," said Monte. "Kinda wanted to be sure who it was, Lavelle. Let's go inside."

They were only partly dressed, and the night air was cold.

Brent Allard had heard them talking, and now he lighted the lamp. They came and sat down.

"All right," said Lavelle. "They brought Red to town and turned him over to a doctor. I'd like to know what it was all about."

Monte swore softly.

"He ain't dead, Lavelle?"

"He's not far from it, Monte."

"Well, it was Red's own fault. We got a few drinks, and Red wanted to go out and throw a scare into them two punchers at the Triangle-D; so we –"

"What was the idea of the scare?" interrupted Lavelle.

"Well, it was like this. Brent heard about these two punchers bein' out there, and Brent got scared right away. You go ahead and tell him about it, Brent."

"There ain't much to tell," said Brent Allard. "I told the boys to look out for these two. I just happen to know that they're bad medicine for anybody to monkey with. The gang all laughed at me when I said that

146

Hartley was the most dangerous man in the country.

"I told Red to let 'em alone, but he told me I was a coward. By golly, I knew. But Red said we'd have some fun; so we went to town –"

"You used to know Hartley, did you, Allard?"

"Yeah, I knew him. I know of some deals he pulled off, and I'd rather have the small-pox around me. Anyway, Red had an idea that we could throw a scare into 'em. He thought, mebbe, that Bud Daley would be there; so he was goin' to try and find out.

"Red's idea was for all of us to pack a rope and surround the place. He was goin' to sneak up and make a noise near the front door. Not a big noise, but just enough to wake 'em up. We were to be ready with the ropes and –"

"Red was goin' to put a loop of rope at the front door," interjected Mesa.

"Red had it all figured out," Brent spat disgustedly. "We was goin' to make believe we was goin' to hang 'em. Red's idea was to scare 'em. Anyway, it worked out up to the place where Red sneaked up close to a window. A man came from the stable and told Red to put up his hands.

"Red started shootin' and this man downed him. We started shootin' at this man, and he
147

faded out in the dark. Well, we didn't know what else to do; so we beat it for home."

Lavelle frowned heavily. "Any idea who this man was?"

"I'd bet a horse it was Hartley," said Brent Allard.

"Laying for you?"

"How would he know we were comin'?" Thus Mesa.

"I told you fellers –"

"You make me sick!" snorted Monte.

"All right, all right. If Red had listened to me, he wouldn't be at the doctor's office now."

Lavelle smiled grimly as he studied Allard's face.

"You're rather afraid of Hartley, eh?"

"Oh, hell, what's the use?" Allard shut his lips and began manufacturing a cigarette.

Lavelle got to his feet and turned toward the door.

"I've got to beat it back. Keep your mouths shut, all of you. None of you know what Red was doing there to-night. He was a fool for going, and he probably got what was coming to him."

"You can fix it with Breed, can'tcha?" asked Monte.

"There's nothing to fix. Breed won't worry much about it. He'll let it drop."

148

"Suppose Red talks in his sleep?" Allard looked up at Lavelle anxiously.

"We'll have to take that chance. Good-night."

One of their horses was missing in the morning, but Bud took his own saddle. Sleepy saddled one of the buggy team and found it a much better riding than harness animal. They went to Modoc, where they found that Red Blair was still unconscious and that the doctor was still prospecting him for bullets.

Dug Breed made a show of questioning Hashknife, while Cleve Lavelle listened. But Hashknife had told all he knew the night before. Lavelle was thoughtfully serious, and the bartender confided to Hashknife that Lavelle had lost a lot of money at stud poker last night.

"And that's the first time anybody has tapped him hard since Bud Daley took ten thousand out of here," stated the bartender.

"Lost his luck?" queried Hashknife, grinning.

"I betcha." The bartender breathed tenderly upon a glass, and polished it carefully.

"Lavelle's sure out of luck when they can hit him hard."

"Gamblin' is a queer profession," mused
149

Hashknife. "They're all superstitious. They make up their mind that somethin' brings 'em luck – and it does. I reckon it's just another case of mind."

"Lavelle's thataway," laughed the bartender. "Horse-shoes, pins on the floor pointin' toward him, pictures hangin' crooked on the wall – oh, a lot of hoodoo or good-lucks."

"Alle same Injun medicine-bag, eh?" grinned Sleepy.

"That's it."

Lavelle came in and walked over to the bar, inviting the two cowboys to have a drink.

"How far is it to Black Wells?" asked Hashknife as they lifted their glasses.

"About thirty-five miles," said Lavelle.

"Good road?"

"Good enough for a saddle-horse. Been neglected so long that it wouldn't be passable for a wagon. Thinking of going there?"

Hashknife nodded slowly.

"Yeah, I'm goin' over there, Lavelle. Have you got any idea what could have become of Bud Daley's cattle?"

Lavelle laughed and indicated for the bartender to fill up the glasses again.

"Just between us," said Lavelle, "I think that Bud sold his cattle."

"In Black Wells?"

"Perhaps. That is the best place."

"Well," said Hashknife, "we're goin' over there and see what we can see. There ought to be somebody there that could put us on to the right track."

"If they would. Black Wells," said Lavelle slowly, "is one place where it's hard to get folks to talk."

"We never get folks to talk," said Hashknife. "Let 'em alone and they'll tell you everythin'. Well, Sleepy, we better be hittin' the grit. We've got to stop at the JM outfit a while, and I dunno if them hammer-headed broncs are good for thirty-five miles or not."

"You two were on the car the night the hold-up men took Bud away from the sheriff, wasn't you?" asked Lavelle.

"Y'betcha," grinned Hashknife. "I'll never forget it. They tried to rob me and Sleepy, but I told 'em that all we had left was the draggin' end of a pair of railroad tickets, so he dug into his pocket and tossed me some money for a breakfast stake."

Lavelle laughed and lighted a cigar.

"How much did he give you?"

"I dunno. It wasn't much. Well, c'mon, Sleepy, let's hit the grit."

Monte Sells and Frank Asher were riding into town, as Hashknife and Sleepy rode out.

Monte squinted closely at them and turned in his saddle to watch them fade out down the road in a cloud of dust.

The Miller family, Mrs. Daley and the cowpunchers were all at the JM and greeted them warmly. Sody noticed that Sleepy was riding one of Bud's horses, and asked him what was wrong with the JM horse.

"Bud took him," laughed Hashknife. "From what we can observe, Bud has a horse, grub, and a gun. He took that rifle out of the corner of the front room, cleaned out the cupboard, and lifted a horse."

"Oh, did you see him – talk to him?" exclaimed Mrs. Daley.

"Wish I had," said Hashknife. "We wasn't there when he came. We was packin' Red Blair to a doctor."

"What happened to Red Blair?" asked Uncle Jimmy.

Hashknife described what had happened at the ranch the night before, and Dinah Blewette almost choked to death trying to express himself. Sody hammered him on the back and ordered him to use his ears and let his tongue alone.

"Do you suppose that Bud had anything to do with it?" asked Mrs. Daley wonderingly.

"He didn't have no gun," said Sleepy.

"Least, we don't reckon he did. It was after that when he took the rifle."

"Well, tie up yore horses and have somethin' to eat," invited Ma Miller. "You two gallinippers are just like every other puncher I ever knowed – always show up at meal time."

"Ma throws a mean flock of food," grinned Uncle Jimmy. "I know she's bakin' bread and there's beans in the oven, too."

"Oh, we'll stay," said Hashknife. "My gosh, we'll stay."

The wide porch of the ranch-house looked inviting to Hashknife. Sody and Dinah were breaking a bronc at the corral, and this was inviting enough for Sleepy. Uncle Jimmy followed Ma to the kitchen, leaving Hashknife and Mrs. Daley together. They sat down in the shade, and Mrs. Daley waited for Hashknife to speak. His long, lean face was serious as he carefully rolled and shaped a cigarette before saying a word. Then:

"Where was you the night the bank was robbed?"

"Why, I was at home."

Mrs. Daley looked curiously at him, and a fear clutched at her heart. Did he know that Cleve Lavelle was out at the ranch that night, she wondered?

"Wasn't Bud home that night?" he asked.

She shook her head slowly.

"No, he did not come home."

"Where'd he go that day – to Modoc?"

"I – I think so. He said he was going to see the sheriff about the stolen cattle."

"Uh-huh." Hashknife smoked thoughtfully. "Are him and Breed good friends?"

"No, I do not think so."

Hashknife turned and looked directly at her as he said, –

"Lavelle thinks that Bud sold his cows and lied about 'em being stolen."

"That is not true! Why, Bud wouldn't do a thing like that. You ought to know Bud better –"

"I didn't say it," interrupted Hashknife. "Lavelle said it."

"Well, it's not true. We were just getting a good start in life when this all happened."

"All right," Hashknife nodded and shoved his hat on to the back of his head. "Why didn't Bud talk at the trial?"

"Why didn't he talk?" Mrs. Daley looked at Hashknife closely.

"Yeah. He didn't even try to tell where he was that night."

"No, he didn't tell," Mrs. Daley spoke softly. "He wouldn't tell anything."

"Feller ought to talk," said Hashknife

154

slowly. "Did he ever tell you that he didn't do it, May?"

"No." Softly.

"Did he ever tell you where he was that night?"

"No."

"Say!"

Hashknife turned half around and looked at her. She lowered her eyes, but he put his hand on her shoulder and she looked up at him, her eyes filmed with tears.

"May Daley, did Bud talk to you a-tall?"

She bit her lips to try to keep back the tears, as she shook her head.

"Why didn't he?"

"I – I do not know."

"Grub-pile!" yelled Uncle Jimmy. "Come and git it!"

Hashknife helped her to her feet and she gripped his hand tightly as she looked up at him.

"Why do you ask me these questions?"

Hashknife grinned down at her and shook his head.

"I can't tell yuh yet, May. I don't want yuh to think that I'm meddlin' into yore personal affairs; but I'd like to ask yuh if yuh still care for Bud?"

"More than any one in the world, Hashknife Hartley."

Hashknife nodded slowly.

"I hope he knows that, May. If I wasn't his friend I'd think he was guilty; but friendship makes it look different."

"Do you –" she faltered – "do you think there is any way of saving him?"

Hashknife grinned and patted her on the arm.

"Miracles do happen," he told her smiling. "I saved half of my salary one year. Let's eat and forget it."

CHAPTER XIV

The town of Black Wells was on the east side of the range and on the main line of the railroad, the branch of which extended into the Modoc country, but from a point much farther south.

Until the building of this branch line all the cattle of the Modoc had been herded into Black Wells for shipment; but since then Black Wells had ceased to be more than one of the many little cattle towns along the railroad.

Its one street was little more than a dusty road, bordered by false-fronted, unpainted buildings, which looked as if they might fall down in the next gust of wind; their signs were faded and dimmed by time.

The railroad did not come within a quarter of a mile of the town and it seemed that the town did not like the railroad well enough to move over close to it. The little depot stood bravely forth in the sage-covered plain, and a few hundred yards from it were the big corrals and loading-pens, fast falling apart from neglect.

Hashknife and Sleepy rode into Black Wells after dark, put their horses into a corral, foraged some hay and went hunting for a hotel. A frowsy hotel-keeper answered their banging on the front door, grumbled at being disturbed, but finally agreed to give them a place to sleep.

He held up his overalls with one hand, a smoking oil lamp in the other, and padded along barefooted to a door, which creaked a protest at being disturbed.

"Ain't used to puttin' up folks at night," he explained. "The hotel business ain't what it used to be. I've seen the time when this old Californy House was loaded to the guards. I'll leave yuh fix up the bed the way yuh want it. This lamp ain't got more'n enough ile to see yuh to bed, and I'll be darned 'f I'd ever fill one by match-light."

157

He placed the lamp on a rickety dresser and peered around.

"How about a little water, pardner?" asked Hashknife.

"Water? T'night? Nope." He shook his head violently. "Fetch yuh some in the mornin'. That darn old pump is hard t' find in the dark, and she's gotta be primed to beat hell, or yuh don't git nothin' to come up."

He padded out, shut the door, and went down the narrow hallway, complaining audibly. The room was hot, unventilated; but both cowboys were too tired to care about that. They flopped on the old bed, which creaked and groaned at every move, and stayed there until daylight, when they went wearily down the hall and on to the front porch.

Black Wells woke up by degrees. A mongrel dog got up from in front of the Welcome saloon, turned round three times, lay down. Then it got up, yawned widely, snapped at a fly, and went down the street toward a watering-trough.

Somewhere a door banged shut, and some one began whistling discordantly. A high-pitched voice complained profanely against the whistler, who stopped whistling long enough to tell the plaintiff to go plumb to

158

hell. A window slammed down and there came a tinkle of broken glass.

"You blame fool, that winder has been cracked ever since eighteen eighty-six!" complained a feminine voice. "Watcha slammin' it down fer?"

The reply was muffled. A man came across the street leading a horse to the watering-trough. He began manipulating the rusty old pump-handle, which screeched loud enough to wake every one. Another man came out of a one-story building across the street; a short dumpy man, bearded to the eyes. He slid back the wide door of the black-smith shop and went inside, where he busied himself singing a tuneless song and beating time on the anvil. The proprietor of the hotel, evidently fearful that Hashknife and Sleepy might get away without paying for their lodging, came out on to the porch, still using his two hands in lieu of suspenders.

"Howja sleep?" he asked.

"With our eyes shut," said Hashknife.

"Howja find the bed?"

"That wasn't a bed," said Sleepy dryly, "that was a buggy."

The man seemed aggrieved.

"Yuh can't expect no New York accommodations in Black Wells. Hell, man; yo're in the West. Black Wells

is a good town. Whatcha like for breakfast —
coffee or tea?"

Hashknife laughed and got to his feet.

"That's what I've always heard about Black
Wells — yuh can get what yuh want. We'll take
coffee."

"Yuh sure can git anythin' yuh want,"
admitted the proprietor. "She's a he-man's
town, y'betcha."

He went back into the house. The blacksmith was still singing to the music of his
anvil, his voice quavering with the intensity
of feeling. Hashknife grinned and nodded
toward the shop.

"That feller's human, Sleepy. My bronc
has a loose shoe; so we'll give the singer a job,
and mebbe he'll talk."

They got the horse at the corral and took
it to the shop. The blacksmith grinned good-
naturedly and examined the loose shoe.

"Better take her off and shape her up li'l,
eh?" he asked.

"Yo're the doctor," said Hashknife. "Do
yore job."

"Quite a town yuh got here," observed
Sleepy.

The blacksmith looked up from his work
and squinted at Sleepy.

"You tryin' to be funny, or start an
argument?" he asked.

"Neither one," grinned Sleepy. "But that's the regular thing to say, ain't it?"

The blacksmith laughed and walked back to his forge, when he shoved the shoe into the fire and leaned heavily on his bellows pole.

"You fellers are strangers here," he said slowly. "I *sabe* the JM brand on this bronc, and I *sabe* the Modoc. I ain't been here long, but I know everybody by their first names. Black Wells is a hell of a town, any old way yuh look at it."

"Ain't much since Modoc quit bringin' their cows over here, I reckon," said Hashknife. "I dunno how yuh make a livin'."

"Oh, I manage to get a little job now and then."

"Know the 76-A outfit?"

"Know of 'em. I put a couple of shoes on a 76-A bronc not long ago. That was the first job I had, after I opened this shop."

"You been open long?"

"Less than a month."

He took the shoe from the fire and shaped it carefully, while Hashknife sat on the edge of the slack-tub and watched him work.

"You must 'a' been here when them Triangle-D cows were brought over here," said Hashknife thoughtfully. "That wasn't more than a month ago."

161

The blacksmith squinted thoughtfully for a moment.

"No, I don't remember them. Mebbe that was before my time. Who owned them Triangle-D cattle?"

"Bud Daley."

"Oh, yeah. He was the feller that robbed the Modoc bank, wasn't he? And then got away from the sheriff?"

"That's the feller."

"I dunno him. How did he happen to bring his cows over here?"

Hashknife laughed shortly and shook his head.

"Do you know the sheriff of Modoc?"

"Nope." The blacksmith went over to the horse and fitted the shoe. "I dunno many folks over there. I used to be there a couple of years ago, but I went up to Pocatello, Idaho, and stayed there until jist a while ago."

"Over in Modoc they told me that Black Wells has a pretty bad reputation," said Hashknife, watching the blacksmith closely.

"I dunno." The blacksmith laughed shortly and came back to the forge. "I never seen anythin' bad about it. I suppose there's a certain gang that ain't teachin' no Sunday schools; but they jist kinda fade in and fade out of here. Nobody bothers me; so I keep my mouth shut and drive nails."

162

"After all," observed Hashknife, "that's the best thing to do."

"Safest, anyway," grunted the blacksmith.

The proprietor of the hotel came out on the porch, a huge bell in his hand, and proceeded to announce breakfast. Men began to drift in from all directions, and there was a sizable crowd in the dining-room when Hashknife and Sleepy arrived.

No one spoke to them, but, being strangers, they created a certain amount of silent interest. Hashknife sized up the crowd and decided that Black Wells might be able to live up to advance notices. There were two men whose attire stamped them as saloon owners or gamblers, another whose tonsorial splendour shrieked of the fact that he mixed drinks for a livelihood. Another might be a keeper of a store. The rest were cowpunchers or cattlemen.

There was little conversation, except in a low tone. The proprietor of the hotel waited on table, assisted by a slatternly middle-aged woman, who did not change expression during the meal.

After breakfast they filed silently out of the room. Hashknife and Sleepy went back to the blacksmith shop, paid for the work and took their horse back to the corral.

"I wish I knowed what in hell we came

163

down here for," complained Sleepy. "This ain't my idea of a good place to stay."

"I want to find out if Bud sold them cows himself," replied Hashknife.

"All right," grinned Sleepy. "That's somethin' yuh never did expect to find out down here."

"You'd laugh at me if I told yuh why I came, Sleepy."

"No, I'd fall dead, Hashknife."

They went into the Welcome saloon, where a poker game had already started. Hashknife looked the players over, but decided that there was too much dexterity shown by the dealer; so he did not take the vacant chair. The blacksmith came in, bought himself a drink and appropriated the chair.

Several hard-faced cowpunchers drifted in, took a few drinks and went away. It was hot. The old saloon reeked of stale liquor and tobacco smoke. Flies crawled over the bar and buzzed up and down the dusty mirror and windows.

The proprietor of the saloon, a crafty-faced individual, with an almost bald head, which was knobby in contour, was in the poker game. He drank whisky copiously and perspired generously on his bald dome.

The day passed slowly, dustily. The poker game was listless, and Hashknife and Sleepy

164

dozed in a pair of chairs on the porch of the saloon. Cow-ponies stood listlessly at the hitch-racks, switching their tails wearily at the flies, while the sun beat down on the dusty street until the pine boards of the buildings oozed pitch.

"There ain't been a soul spoke to us all day," said Sleepy. "I hope to gosh that we pull out this evenin'. Even if they do use our dooryard to pull off their killin's, I'd rather be there than here."

Supper time came and about the same crowd went to eat. There was a little more conversation, because of the fact that much liquor had been consumed. Several of the men nodded to Hashknife and Sleepy, and the proprietor of the Welcome muttered something about it being a warm day for this time of year.

"They're thawin' out," grinned Hashknife.

"At a hundred and ten in the shade, they ought to," grunted Sleepy, wrinkling up his nose at the dishes of hot food. "I'd like to hit that old Crooked Cañon ag'in. It's cool there."

"Don't get impatient," said Hashknife. "Rome wasn't built in a day."

"Oh, that's what yo're doin' over here, eh? Buildin' another Rome."

They went back to the Welcome saloon and

165

sat down. Men drifted in and started another poker game, but this time the proprietor of the saloon did not sit in at the games. He went behind the bar and let the bartender go to eat his supper, and his first act was to invite everybody up to have a drink.

Hashknife and Sleepy came up with the others, but stayed at the bar after the rest of the crowd had gone back to their drinks.

"You fellers goin' to locate around here?" asked the proprietor.

He had drunk enough whisky to make him just a trifle thick of tongue, but his eyes were keen.

Hashknife considered his question thoughtfully, but finally shook his head.

"Didja come from over in the Modoc country?"

The man was busy washing glasses and did not look up when he asked the question.

"Yeah, we rode in from there last night," yawned Hashknife.

The proprietor filled several bottles from a keg, arranged his glasses carefully and turned back to them.

"Many Modoc folks drift over this way?" queried Hashknife.

The man appeared interested in an argument which had started at one of the poker tables, and did not answer, although

166

Hashknife felt sure that he had heard the question. Finally he said:

"When are you goin' back to Modoc?"

"Mebbe to-night, we dunno," said Hashknife.

"Nicer ridin' at night than in the daytime."

The man looked straight at them when he spoke, and it seemed that his statement held a warning.

"That's right," grinned Hashknife. "It's kinda hot in the daytime. You know much about the Modoc country?"

"Not much."

Hashknife leaned across the bar and lowered his voice.

"Pardner, I'm lookin' for information. Do you know who Bud Daley is?"

The man squinted keenly at him, but lowered his eyes, a slight frown on his face. He was putting up a show of thinking. Then:

"I've heard the name. Didn't he git into trouble over there?"

"They say he shipped some stock from here," said Hashknife, ignoring the question, "and we're tryin' to find out if that is the truth."

The man shook his head, but called to a cowpuncher who was watching one of the games. He was a frowsy, unkempt individual,

167

who had been around there all day. He slouched over to the bar.

"Jud," said the proprietor, "here's a man who wants to find out if Bud Daley has shipped any stock from here lately."

Jud licked his lips and reached for a cigarette paper.

"Jud kinda has charge of the loadin' corrals," explained the proprietor.

"Bud Daley?" Jud seemed to be questioning himself. Then he looked at Hashknife keenly. "Whatcha want to know fer?"

"I'll trade answers with yuh," said Hashknife.

"Trade with me?"

"Yeah. You tell me if he has and I'll tell yuh what I wanted to know for."

Jud grinned wisely and licked the edge of his cigarette paper. His eyes shifted to the face of the proprietor and back to Hashknife.

"Suppose I tell yuh I don't know," he suggested. "How'd yuh trade on that?"

"By tellin' yuh it wasn't none of yore damn business," replied Hashknife.

Jud gawped at Hashknife for a moment and flushed angrily.

"Yo're kinda salty, ain't yuh?" he queried.

Hashknife laughed with his mouth, but there was no mirth to his steady eyes. Jud

168

fidgeted nervously, ripped a match viciously along the bar and lit his cigarette.

"I'll buy a drink," said the proprietor slowly.

Jud whirled on his heel and walked back to the poker table, ignoring the invitation. The proprietor laughed and set out glasses and a bottle. He did not drink, but lighted a fresh cigar instead.

"This one is on me," said Hashknife, tossing a dollar on the bar. "I reckon that folks didn't lie to us when they said that we'd never find out anythin' in Black Wells."

He and Sleepy tossed off their drinks and went outside, leaving the dollar on the bar.

"My gosh, that's awful whisky!" exclaimed Sleepy. "No wonder this town hates itself. Where now?"

"Back to Modoc," said Hashknife, "I don't like this place."

They went back to the corral and began saddling. A moon had just come up over the Modoc hills. Sleepy was fussing with his cinch and looking at the moon. Then he stopped and grasped the saddle with both hands.

The moon was acting queerly. It seemed to advance and recede rapidly, and the queer motion was making Sleepy sea-sick. He looked over at Hashknife, who seemed to

169

be acting strangely. Then a sudden dizziness struck him and he fell backward against the corral fence, where he slumped down in a heap.

It seemed to Sleepy that he had only been on the ground a short time, when he groped for the fence and managed to get back to his feet. The moon was high in the heavens now, and he wondered how it had got up there in such a short time. He was still nauseated, hazy; but the cool night breeze revived him rapidly.

The horses were still there. He crossed the corral, where he found Hashknife leaning against the fence, his head on his hands.

"Say, what in hell happened?" queried Sleepy painfully.

Hashknife groaned and straightened up. He looked at Sleepy and laughed hoarsely.

"Feel in yore pockets, Sleepy."

Sleepy did so.

"Anythin' missin'?" asked Hashknife.

"Well, I'll be darned if I ain't shy about ten dollars!"

"They cleaned me out," groaned Hashknife. "I'm as clean as a new six-gun barrel."

"Well, what in hell is the answer?" demanded Sleepy angrily.

"Them last drinks," said Hashknife, "they

170

must 'a' filled 'em full of knockout drops, Sleepy. I've been doped before, but I never got all there was in the world in one drink. Waugh!"

"They doped and robbed us?" queried Sleepy.

"That's the answer."

"All right." Sleepy's voice was harsh with anger. "We'll go back to that Welcome saloon and take it back with interest. C'mon, Hashknife. I'll show that bunch of tin-horns somethin' quaint."

"Nope." Hashknife laughed and went back to his horse. "Me and you are goin' back to Modoc. It's late."

"You ain't goin' to let that bunch of side-winders get away with all this, are yuh?" demanded Sleepy.

"They didn't get much."

Sleepy went to his horse, shook up the saddle and drew up the cinch. He was mad. They rode out of the corral gate and down the street. As they passed the Welcome saloon, Sleepy drew up his horse and peered through the window. There were several men at the bar and among them was the proprietor.

"Hang on to yourself," advised Hashknife. But he was too late.

Sleepy drew his gun and sent a bullet smashing through the window and into the back bar. The crowd at the bar fell back in a panic. Another bullet bored through the broken window, splintered the back-bar mirror and played havoc with some bottled goods which were on display.

A man threw open the door, but slammed it shut quickly, when a bullet buzzed in over his head.

"Yeow! Ye-e-e-ow!" whooped Sleepy. "Dodge, you Black Wells pickpockets!"

Three times more he sent bullets in through the windows before he set spurs to his horse and went thundering out of Black Wells, riding high in his saddle and stuffing more cartridges into his six-shooter.

Straight out the old Crooked Cañon road they went, and into the moonlit hills before they slackened pace.

"I sure gave 'em a receipt for my money!" laughed Sleepy, looking back toward the town, "yo're too easy, Hashknife. I only hope that bunch of reptiles will be pickin' glass splinters out of their mangy hides for a month."

"Well," laughed Hashknife, "I dunno that I blame yuh, cowboy."

"Blame, hell!" snorted Sleepy, "I wish we'd 'a' gone in there and salivated the whole works. I was shootin' at the cash register, and I hope I rung up enough to make it worth

172

while. You wanted to come to Black Wells, and I hope you're satisfied."

"I'm satisfied," answered Hashknife. "Perfectly satisfied."

"You didn't do no good for anybody."

"Didn't I?"

"Well, where in hell did yuh? You asked questions and got no answer. We got doped and robbed. And you're satisfied. Brother, it don't take much to satisfy you, does it? Sometimes I wonder if you're just right in the head."

"My heart is in the right place, Sleepy."

"Yeah – and I suppose yore liver is accordin' to the location notice. You're actin' as happy as though you done some good there."

But Hashknife only laughed joyfully, in spite of the fact that his stomach was almost too weak to bear the drag of his heavy belt and gun.

CHAPTER XV

It was breakfast time the next morning at the 76-A when Dug Breed and Charley Morse rode in for breakfast. A rumour that Bud

Daley was back in the Lost Pine country had given them eighteen hours of riding, with no results.

Monte Sells, Frank Asher, and Brent Allard were eating, but stopped long enough to greet the sheriff and deputy, who sat down at the long table.

"A feller don't have to strain his eyesight to see that yuh didn't have much luck, sheriff," observed Monte.

He winked at the other two cowboys. Dug Breed noted the wink, but did not appreciate the humour of Monte's observation.

"Not much," said Breed dryly.

Frank Asher laid down his fork, rested his elbows on the table and leaned toward Breed, as he said, –

"Breed, who do you think shot Red Blair?"

The sheriff had a cup of hot coffee at his lips, but he slowly lowered it to the table, his eyes searching the faces of the three men across the table.

"What in hell was Blair doin' out there?" he countered.

"What's that got to do with it?" asked Monte.

"Quite a lot." The sheriff seemed more at ease. "If we knew what Red Blair was doin' out there, we might get a line on who shot him."

174

Asher grunted and began eating, but Monte took up the discussion.

"What do yuh know about them two punchers who are livin' at Bud's place?"

"Not a thing."

"Did yuh ever think that they might've had a hand in the shootin' of Red?"

"If you'll tell me what Red was doin' out there, I might say."

Brent Allard got to his feet and shoved back his chair.

"What's the use of arguin' about it?" he asked.

"I'm not arguin' about it," laughed Breed. "Red will likely tell us what he was doin' out there as soon as he is able."

"The doctor don't think he'll get well," observed Monte. "I was down there last night. Them two punchers told about a lot of shots bein' fired out there that night. They claim to have found Red after the shootin' was all over."

Breed nodded slowly.

"Yeah, I know that's what they said."

"Who do yuh reckon done all the shootin'?" queried Allard.

"Didn't you say that there wasn't no use arguin' about it?" asked Breed, grinning. "Don't ask me who done it, Allard; I didn't see 'em."

Breed and Morse finished their breakfast and went on to town, while the three cowboys sat down on the ranch-house porch and rolled fresh cigarettes.

"Do yuh know what I think?" asked Monte.

Nobody seemed to care what he thought, but he continued, –

"I think that Bud Daley was the one that shot Red."

"All right," said Brent Allard. "It's a free country, Monte. I told yuh before we went there that we was monkeyin' with dynamite. But Red got a lot of drinks under his belt –"

"He didn't get any more than the rest of us did," interrupted Monte.

"I know it. But Red got braver than the rest of us. I told yuh what would happen. Red thought we could frame up a scare for them two jaspers, but yuh see what happened, don't yuh?"

"Aw-w-w, hell!" snorted Frank Asher. "You can't make me believe that one of them was guardin' the place. They didn't know we was comin' out there. I'll betcha that Bud was the one what busted up the party for Red."

"Here comes Mesa," said Monte, pointing down the road, where a lone horseman was riding swiftly toward the ranch.

176

They watched him ride in at the gate and come straight to the porch, where he dismounted and joined them.

"Red died a couple of hours ago," he stated wearily. "He never got conscious."

Monte swore softly and rolled a fresh cigarette, while Mesa Caldwell helped himself to Monte's tobacco.

"Lavelle thinks it was Bud Daley that done it," said Mesa. "I was talkin' to Lavelle a while ago. Met the sheriff and his deputy and told them about it. I reckon most everybody thinks that Bud done the shootin'."

"That's where yo're all wrong," insisted Brent Allard. "If you poor fools would only believe me when I tell yuh that them two fellers, Hartley and Stevens, are —"

"Aw, stop croakin', Brent!" wailed Monte. "My gawd, yo're always lookin' for spooks! If yo're so scared of them two, why don'tcha pull yore freight out of here?"

"Gimme my time, then," said Brent quickly. "I'm plumb willin' to go, Monte. I tell yuh, there ain't nothin' but trouble where yuh find them two snake-hunters. I remember the time they —"

"Aw, hire a hall!" exploded Frank Asher, and Allard subsided, growling and shaking his head.

"So Lavelle thinks that Bud Daley shot

Red, does he?" queried Monte. "I wonder if Lavelle thinks that his opinions are worth a hell of a lot? They'd have a sweet time convicting Bud of it, wouldn't they? Personally, I think the least said about it the better it will be for all of us. Bud's likely got a horse and a gun by this time, and he'll be a hard jigger to corral."

"We'll likely find out," grinned Mesa knowingly. "Lavelle is goin' to turn us all over to the sheriff – to assist him in gettin' Bud Daley."

The three cowboys stared at Mesa, who seemed to enjoy their silent expressions.

"Mesa Caldwell, are you lyin' to us?" demanded Monte.

"Cross m' heart and hope t' die if I am. The country is offerin' two thousand for Bud, dead or alive, and the bank antes a thousand. As soon as our friend Dug Breed gets back to Modoc, Lavelle is goin' to offer him our services."

"Well," said Brent Allard slowly, "Cleve Lavelle and Dug Breed can go plumb to hell, as far as I'm concerned."

Allard set his jaw tightly and hitched up his belt.

"Scared?" queried Mesa, grinning.

"Yeah, I'm scared."

"Of one man?"

178

"No, not of one man. Bud Daley don't count. I liked Bud and I still like him. Them two punchers –"

"Aw, they've got yore goat," laughed Monte, and the other two punchers joined in the laugh at Allard's fears.

"All right." Allard was not interested in the sarcasm.

He knew what he knew, and their joking would not change him.

"They ain't got nothin' to do with us," pointed out Mesa.

"Not until we try to put the deadwood on Bud Daley," agreed Allard. "They're friends of Bud Daley, that's a cinch; and I don't intend to give them a chance to work agin' me. I'll take my pay and hunt for another range – it's safer."

"You won't find a safer place to work than for Lavelle." Thus Monte, who did not want to lose Allard.

"Mebbe we better go over and have a talk with these bad *hombres*," suggested Mesa, laughing. "Would they recognise yuh, Brent?"

Allard squinted at Mesa, but did not answer. He was not going to commit himself.

"We could ride over there," continued Mesa. "It would be four against two. It wouldn't be hard to start somethin',

179

especially if they recognised you and made some remarks."

"Any ti-i-ime," drawled Allard, shaking his head quickly. "Not for mine, Mesa. You fellers trot right along and start somethin' with them two; but leave me here. Mebbe they'd recognise me. Hartley, the tall one, ain't got a bad memory for faces. And –" Allard squinted seriously and rubbed his stubbled chin – "I'd like to bet that he knows more about why and how things have been done since he showed up than the men that done 'em."

"Yo're crazy," declared Monte.

"Jist like a li'l fox," grinned Allard. "I love my own hide so much that I'll go into a hole any old time that the runnin' ain't good."

"Well," observed Mesa, "mebbe yo're right, Brent. If yuh feel like yo're runnin' into bad luck, it's a good thing to lay off the game for a while. Talkin' about luck, Lavelle got a trimmin' at stud agin' last night. Sody Slavin and a gambler from Burke sure cleaned out Lavelle.

"Sody went in on a shoe-string and came out with enough to buy a train load of cows. Lavelle almost lost his shirt. That bird from Burke and Sody took turns throwin' the hook into Lavelle, and I'm tellin' you that the Rest Ye All is danged badly bent."

180

"They must 'a' been loaded with luck," observed Monte. "Lavelle is usually awful lucky at his own game. But he's been gettin' hit hard lately. I wonder if his luck is slippin'?"

"Sure, it's slippin'." Brent Allard spoke with conviction. "The minute I heard them two names I knew –"

"You poor fool!" Monte swung around angrily. "What in creation would they have to do with Cleve Lavelle's luck? You talk like a sick buzzard, Brent."

"He's sure superstitious," laughed Mesa.

But there was a note of uneasiness in Mesa's voice. He, too, believed in omens.

"I dunno," continued Mesa. "Somethin' is wrong with Lavelle's luck – and Lavelle knows it, too. He's sour-balled, I tell yuh. I watched him playin', and he was as nervous as an old woman. Kept kinda lickin' his lips. He got sore at Sody Slavin, 'cause Sody kidded him about his bad luck. Why, I even seen Lavelle kinda countin' his chips."

"Countin' his chips, eh?" grunted Allard. "That's a jinx."

"Mebbe," said Monte thoughtfully, "he was workin' one jinx against the other. Sometimes that works."

Which proved that Monte Sells was not proof against superstition. Brent Allard

181

laughed at Monte's opinion and stalked off the porch toward the bunk-house.

"Damn him!" muttered Monte, after Allard had passed out of earshot. "Him and his crazy superstition make me tired. We'll all be jumpin' around with bad nerves if he don't quit it."

"Well, let's go and take a look at these two pelicans," suggested Mesa. "We don't have to choose 'em, if we don't want to."

And while the boys of the 76-A argued about them, Hashknife and Sleepy rode in at the JM ranch in time for breakfast. Sody Slavin, with wealth in every pocket, greeted them like long-lost brothers and insisted on telling them how he had helped clean out Cleve Lavelle.

"It was like takin' straw away from the crippled cow," explained Sody. "I seen him quit cold, when he had me beat in sight. And I went in with ten dollars. Man, I never seen a game like that. I'd take a wallop at Lavelle and then that gambler from Burke would paste him for a bushel of chips. We sure see-sawed him out of a lot of *dinero*."

"Yuh ought to have a little compassion," said Hashknife.

"Not me." Sody shook his head. "I hookum cow, when I git m' feet rammed into a lucky spot. Lavelle has cleaned me

182

plenty of times, but I'm more'n even with him this time."

Ma Miller welcomed them to breakfast and demanded the latest news from Black Wells.

"I used to know Black Wells pretty well," she laughed. "When we used to trail our cows over there, I handled the chuck-wagon."

"And there never was a puncher late for a meal," declared Uncle Jimmy proudly. "Ma sure can make food. Black Wells ain't much, is she?"

"Not much," grinned Hashknife. "This here food don't look like what they feed yuh over there."

"They didn't like us," grinned Sleepy, balancing a whole fried egg on his knife-blade. "They don't fuss over strangers."

Sody grinned encouragingly. He felt that something worth while had happened over there and wondered how they had found out that Black Wells did not like them. Mrs. Daley came from upstairs and smiled a welcome to them. She sat down at the table and waited for the conversation to resume.

"Do any of you folks know a puncher over there named Jud? He's kinda pointed-faced, with squirrel teeth, and looks like he never lived in a country where there was soap."

"That's Jud Mahley," said Uncle Jimmy. "I betcha that's who yuh mean. His eyes are awful close together – kinda makes him look like he's cross-eyed."

"That's him," grinned Hashknife. "And there's the proprietor of the Welcome saloon. He's –"

"That's 'Bumpy' Dickenson," laughed Sody. "Got a bald head, with bumps all over it, ain't he?"

"That's the whip-poor-will," admitted Sleepy. "Nice sort of a gent."

"With a reverse-English!" exploded Uncle Jimmy. "There ain't a bigger crook in the world than Dickenson."

"Unless it's Jud Mahley," amended Sody. "He ain't only crooked, but he's lucky."

"Sody shot at him once," grinned Uncle Jim, "and Sody has been sore ever since."

"Danged right!" snorted Sody. "I'd bet forty dollars agin' a cigarette paper that it was Jud Mahley. He was usin' a runnin'-iron on a calf, back toward Crooked Cañon. I had a .45-70 and a lot of them darn D.C. ca'tridges that got into this country because they were cheap.

"Anyway, I got a good runnin' shot at that jasper, and I'd 'a' handed him a harp; but the head blowed off the shell, knocked heck out of my Winchester, and I couldn't see to spit for twenty minutes."

Hashknife laughed at Sody's disgusted
184

expression. He knew just how Sody had felt at the time.

"So Jud used to be over here, eh?" he asked.

"Yeah, he sure did," grunted Sody. "He worked around for the different outfits. Thinks he's a gunman. He sure rattled his hocks out of the Modoc hills."

"Aw, he comes back once in a while," said Uncle Jimmy. "I seen him in Modoc a few weeks ago."

"And yuh didn't tell me?" Sody grew indignant to think that this information had been withheld.

"You still want to kill him?" asked Hashknife.

"Yo're darn right, I do!"

"Well, you've got my permission," laughed Sleepy. "But you've got to beat me to him. I've picked him, cowboy."

They got up from the breakfast table and moved into the living-room, while Ma and Mrs. Daley cleared away the breakfast table.

Uncle Jimmy signalled Hashknife to follow him outside, and they walked to the far corner of the porch.

"Did yuh find out anythin'?" queried Uncle Jimmy.

Hashknife shook his head slowly.

"Nothin' that would show who sold them

cows of Bud's. They're a tight-lipped outfit over there, Uncle Jimmy."

"Shucks, yes," thoughtfully, "I dunno whether we'll ever find out the truth of it all. I hate to think that Bud is guilty."

"I wish to gosh I could have a talk with Bud."

"He wouldn't talk when he was in jail, Hartley."

"He'd talk to me or I'd knock hell out of him."

"Uh-huh." Uncle Jimmy seemed a bit dubious of Hashknife's ability to do this.

"I've got a hunch that Bud's cows were shipped out of Black Wells," said Hashknife, "but that's as far as my hunch goes. This Jud Mahley has charge of the loadin' corrals over there, but he won't talk. Have yuh heard how that Red Blair is gettin' along?"

Uncle Jimmy shook his head. He was not interested in Blair.

"That was kind of a funny deal," observed Hashknife. "Do yuh suppose Bud had anythin' to do with it?"

"I don't think so." Uncle Jimmy sucked thoughtfully on his old pipe. "Red Blair and Bud never had any trouble that I know about."

"Blair works for Lavelle, don't he? Who else is in that outfit?"

186

Uncle Jimmy named over the other cowboys of the 76-A. Hashknife listened thoughtfully, squinting his eyes away from the smoke of his cigarette.

"Brent Allard, eh? Kinda sad-lookin' jasper, with a lock of hair that's always in his eyes?"

"Yeah." Uncle Jimmy looked up quickly. "You know him?"

Hashknife grinned softly and threw away his cigarette.

"I know a Brent Allard, and I'd like to see if this is the one. Does Bud Daley know Jud Mahley?"

"Yeah, he knows him. Everybody around here knows Jud. There's a fat reward out for Bud. The country offers two thousand dollars, dead or alive; and the bank say he's worth a thousand to them."

"That's a lot of money, Uncle Jimmy."

The old man nodded slowly.

"Yeah – dead or alive," he said sadly and jerked his head toward the door. "I ain't told May. She's got enough to worry about without knowin' that the law is willin' to pay for Bud's carcass. I sure feel sorry for her, Hartley. She's jist a kid.

"Her and Bud was jist gittin' a good start when he got hit with all the troubles in the world. I got sore as hell at Bud, 'cause he

187

wouldn't talk to nobody. I went down there and argued with him, but he didn't seem to give a damn what they done to him. Why, that blamed fool seemed pleased when the judge sentenced him."

Uncle Jimmy snorted his disgust and knocked the dottle from his pipe against his spurred heel.

"Wouldn't even talk to May," added Hashknife.

"Not to anybody. It looked bad to the jury. What could a lawyer do in a case like that? They've got to know whether yo're guilty or not, before they can prove that yuh ain't. But they never did know about Bud."

"That's the one big question," observed Hashknife. "If we only knew why he wouldn't talk."

CHAPTER XVI

Hashknife did not get a chance to talk with Mrs. Daley before they left the JM ranch. He and Sleepy had ridden all night and were too weary to think of much except a chance to stretch out and sleep.

They went back to Bud's ranch-house,

stabled and fed their horses and slept until mid-afternoon. Bud had cleaned out their food supply, which had not been replenished; so they decided to go to Modoc and eat.

At the restaurant they heard that Red Blair was dead, but it did not seem to have excited the town greatly. They met the sheriff, who seemed disposed to talk, or rather to ask questions; so they got away from him as gently as possible and went over to the Rest Ye All.

Lavelle was behind the bar talking to the bartender, but turned as they came up. He squinted at them closely and smiled as he placed a bottle and glasses on the bar.

"We'll have some see-gars," said Hashknife, shoving the bottle aside and leaning against the bar.

"That stuff is ten years old," stated Lavelle.

"Let her live to a ripe old age," grinned Hashknife. "We got hold of some bad liquor over at Black Wells, and it kinda cured us of the drink habit. A shot of that stuff is the best temperance lecture I ever attended."

"Strong?" queried Lavelle.

"Well, I took one drink and it affected the moon," grinned Sleepy, "and that's no danged imagination either."

Lavelle laughed and handed out a box of dusty-looking cigars.

"I remember that you said you was going to Black Wells," he said indifferently. "It used to be a wild place a few years ago."

"I'll bet they're wild yet," laughed Sleepy. "I wrote my initials on the back bar of the Welcome saloon with a six-gun."

"You did?"

Lavelle grew interested and would like to have heard more, but Sleepy decided that he had told quite enough. Sleepy dropped his cigar into a cuspidor and began to roll a cigarette.

"Did you hear that Red Blair died?" asked Lavelle.

"Three times," said Hashknife. "First two times I didn't believe it, but three times is a charm. Did he ever wake up?"

Lavelle shook his head. He did not like the way Hashknife treated the subject, but could hardly see where it would be policy to chide him for his attitude.

"There's three thousand reward for Bud Daley."

Hashknife grinned at Lavelle's statement, but suddenly sobered and leaned across the bar toward Lavelle.

"I hear you've lost yore luck, Lavelle?"

Not a muscle of the gambler's face moved for several moments. Then his eyelids twitched slightly and his lips parted.

190

"What do you mean, Hartley?" he asked coldly.

"I just heard that Sody Slavin busted the stud-game last night. I hear that you quit cold, with the best cards in sight."

Lavelle laughed, but without mirth. Hashknife was looking him straight in the eyes, and the gambler turned his head away.

"Well, he didn't break me," he said slowly, "and as far as quitting – I know enough to quit when I'm beat, Hartley."

Hashknife grinned thoughtfully and tossed away his cigar. He knew that Lavelle was mad, and wondered just how far he could go with his baiting. Lavelle had started to go around the end of the bar, when Hashknife turned to him again.

"What's yore particular hoodoo, Lavelle?"

"Hoodoo?" Lavelle stopped and looked queerly at Hashknife. Then he came back.

"What did you mean by that?" he asked softly.

"Yore bad-luck medicine," explained Hashknife, although he knew that Lavelle understood the question.

"I've knowed a lot of superstitious gamblers," continued Hashknife after a moment. "They believed in signs and all that kinda stuff, and I wondered what yore pet hoodoo was, thasall."

191

Lavelle laughed shortly and shook his head.

"Not me, Hartley. I believe in good luck and bad luck, but I have no charms to bring me luck."

"No, I didn't think yuh did," said Hashknife.

Lavelle looked quickly at him, but did not reply. Sleepy was itching to know what it was all about, but he knew, deep down in his heart, that Hashknife was not talking in vain. Lavelle walked from behind the bar and went toward the back room without another word, while Hashknife laughed silently and rested his elbows on the bar.

A moment later Monte Sells, Frank Asher, Mesa Caldwell and Brent Allard came rattling their spurs and arguing over the fact that the sheriff wanted them to start on their man-hunt today. Monte glanced quickly at Hashknife and Sleepy and stepped aside to see what Brent Allard would do.

Brent was in the rear, crowding in behind Caldwell, who also stepped aside, leaving Brent almost within reach of Hashknife. He looked up and stopped in his tracks. No one spoke. Brent's two hands had been against Caldwell's back, and they remained in that same position for several moments. Then they slowly relaxed, but he kept them above his belt line.

Hashknife was grinning at him, and a foolish grin came to Brent Allard's lips.

"Hyah, Allard?" said Hashknife easily. "Long time I no see yuh. Wyomin', wasn't it?"

"Uh-huh." Allard wet his lips with a dry tongue and cleared his throat raspingly. "I – I come here from Oklyhomy."

"That's right," nodded Hashknife. "I remember hearin' that the sheriff ran yuh out of Oklahoma. Boot-leggin' to the Injuns, wasn't it, Allard?"

Allard grinned foolishly; Monte snorted disgustedly. He felt that Allard was too frightened to resent an insult. Hashknife's eyes flashed to Monte, considered him coldly for a moment, and turned back to Allard.

"You workin' for the 76-A, ain't yuh, Allard?"

"Yeah. I've been here quite a while, Hartley."

"Wasn't it one of yore outfit that got shot out where we're livin'? We packed him in. We jist found out that he died."

"Yeah," said Monte harshly, "and we're lookin' for the man that shot him."

Hashknife squinted at Monte and at the rest of the 76-A outfit. They shifted uneasily under his steady, half-contemptuous gaze.

They remembered that Allard had declared that Hartley could read their minds, and four pairs of eyes shifted uneasily.

"You're lookin' for that man, are yuh?" queried Hashknife slowly.

"You're damn right!" grunted Monte.

"So are we," declared Hashknife. "Come and have a drink."

The invitation was unexpected. For a moment they hesitated, but only for a moment. They had expected trouble. Allard laughed nervously, but was the first one to reach the bar, where he filled his glass with a shaky hand.

"Here's hopin' we find him," said Hashknife seriously.

"If you're huntin' for him," said Allard nervously, "you won't need hopes."

They drank deeply, except Hashknife and Sleepy, who took cigars. Monte grinned at their choice, but the grin left his face when Hashknife said seriously –

"We was over at Black Wells yesterday, and Jud Mahley told us to give yuh his regards."

"The hell he did!" blurted Monte. "Can'tcha think of anythin' funnier than that to say?"

Hashknife laughed softly and shook his head. He wanted to find if Jud Mahley was a friend of the 76-A boys – and he found out quickly.

"Mahley never meant it," laughed Caldwell.

"We've got a hell of a job ahead of us," said Frank Asher disgustedly. "We're goin' to help the sheriff find Bud Daley."

"That'll be quite a chore, I'd imagine." Hashknife hunched backward against the bar and proceeded to crumble the cigar between his long fingers. "I've knowed Bud a long time, and if he ain't changed, you'll have to bring him in on a stretcher."

"And we ain't got a darn thing agin' him," complained Brent Allard. "The law don't mean nothin'."

"It never did, to you, did it?" laughed Hashknife.

"Aw, you know what I mean," protested Allard. "Bud's all right."

"He's all wrong," said Hashknife. "The danged fool never tried to get away. That bandit had to almost throw him off the train."

The 76-A boys exchanged quick glances, as if questioning each other. Monte half-smiled and moved in a trifle closer. It was evident that he did not want any one, except those immediately concerned, to hear his question.

"You got a good look at the two men who

195

took Bud away from Dug Breed, didn't yuh?" he asked.

Hashknife nodded seriously, but his face broke into a grin.

"Yeah, we got a good look – especially into the muzzle of their guns. They were masked, yuh know."

"I *sabe* that part of it," nodded Monte. "It's kinda hard to describe a masked man. But I thought that mebbe yuh was able to kinda pay attention to their size and – you know what I mean."

"Didn't they say anything'?" asked Allard.

"One of 'em did," said Hashknife. "But I reckon he changed his voice quite a lot. The other one said nothin'. If I remember right, they were both kinda tall. One was kinda skinny – the one that didn't talk – but the other one wasn't fat."

"That's a good description," stated Mesa Caldwell.

"It must 'a' been quite a good-sized gang," observed Sleepy, "and it looks like they intended to take Bud away from the sheriff. They never touched any of the other passengers – never even went into the cars."

Monte scratched his chin thoughtfully and motioned for the bartender to fill up their glasses again.

196

"The express robbery must 'a' been done by tenderfeet," grinned Hashknife. "They never got a cent for their trouble."

"I dunno what they'd expect to get on a branch railroad." Thus Sleepy wisely. "They never carry money."

"Sometimes they do," said Monte. "The mines at Dixon ship bullion from the Kalura, and the money for a big pay-roll comes from the bank at Burke."

"They was probably figurin' on that pay-roll money," observed Hashknife. "Somebody must 'a' got the wrong dope."

"Yeah, they must have," agreed Monte dryly.

In a few minutes Charley Morse came in and told them that Breed was in need of their services. Hashknife and Sleepy watched them all ride out of town heading into the hills, with the intention of looking through the Crooked Cañon country.

CHAPTER XVII

Bud Daley squatted on his heels and roasted the saddle of a cotton-tail rabbit over the coals of his little fire. He had secured enough food at his ranch-house to vary his diet a little, but Bud Daley was getting tired of being an outlaw.

He had not dared to approach any of the ranches to get information as to what was being done to apprehend him. His forced delivery from the hands of the sheriff was as much of a mystery to Bud as it was to the sheriff.

Bud had puzzled over it for a long time, and had finally decided that it was merely a coincidence that the train had been robbed on the night he was to be taken away, and that the robbers, knowing that he was a convicted prisoner, had done what they would want some one to do for them.

"Do unto others," muttered Bud, as he squinted away from the smoke of the fire. "That's right, I reckon. I'm tryin' to do it. It's a funny old world. I can't keep runnin' away all my life.

"And I can't walk back there and throw up my hands. After twenty years in the penitentiary I won't care, I suppose. This country will prob'ly be all farms and little towns; and the cattle will all be gone from the open ranges."

He turned away from the fire and looked down across the Modoc hills, hazy blue in the sunshine; his home country. Somewhere down in those hills were men looking for him; men who had been associated with him. Now they were hunting him down like they would hunt down a calf-killing panther, and with no reason, except that twelve men had declared him guilty of a crime which he had not committed.

Bud wondered what May was doing. He felt sure that she was back at the JM ranch, under the protecting wing of Ma Miller. Strangely enough, he did not hold any ill feelings toward Lavelle.

"May wants nice things," he assured himself, "and Lavelle can give 'em to her. But I don't want to be where I can see and know about it. Same old case of what yuh don't know won't hurt yuh, I reckon."

He held his head in his hands as he reflected, the saddle of rabbit rapidly charring in the little fire. Behind him, standing close to a wild cherry tree, was his horse, drowsing in the shade. Unnoticed by Bud the burning rabbit was sending up a spiral of dark smoke, until a faint gust of wind blew its odours to his nostrils.

He quickly poked it out of the coals, swearing softly at the loss of his meal.

"Got to find me another bunny," he grunted wearily, turning his eyes toward his horse. But his relaxed muscles tightened suddenly and he came to his feet in a single movement.

His horse had thrown up its head, ears erect, and was looking across the cañon, where six riders were grouped together, looking in his direction.

The cover was so heavy that the posse were unable to distinguish Bud nor his horse, but Bud knew they had seen the tell-tale smoke and would investigate. Swiftly he moved to the side of his horse, mounted cautiously, and rode back through the little clump of cherry trees.

But the keen eyes of Dug Breed had caught a flash of him, and the posse spread fan-wise and started across the cañon. They were all well mounted, and knew the hills as well as Bud did.

After leaving the cherry thicket Bud spurred his horse to a gallop. He was not sure that the riders had seen him, but he was taking no chances. Across the fork of his saddle he carried a Winchester rifle and his supply of cartridges was adequate for at least a short battle.

But Bud did not want battle. Six to one was too many for him to consider, and he knew that every man in that posse was a good shot.

He rode over the top of the ridge and down across a wide swale, swinging to the left, intending to lead the posse higher into the hills, where he might be able to play hide-and-seek with them until dark. He realised that they would have an advantage in the valley.

But Bud had started his circling tactics too late. As he swung out of the swale and looked back he saw two riders top the hill behind him. A hasty glance to the right showed two more riders racing through the side of the swale, and he knew that the other two had swung to the left.

They were all several hundred yards away, but coming fast. One of those directly behind him yelled a warning and discharged his gun. It was probably the first time they were sure it was Bud Daley.

"C'mon, bronc!" snapped Bud, and rode directly toward the rim of the cañon. It was a steep descent, but Bud was in no position to pick his trail now. The horse fairly slid to the bottom, dislodging old logs, rocks, and other debris.

Fairly leaping his horse across the deep wash at the bottom he urged it up the opposite side, realising with a groan that the riders of the left side would be able to swing around the head of the cañon and block him from that direction.

He had barely reached the crest when he

201

heard the noisy descent of the two riders behind him. His horse was blowing heavily, but he whirled it to the right and galloped along the cañon rim.

"Trapped!" he gritted. "Trapped like a tenderfoot! The two on the right will come through on that old cattle trail, and they'll have me cinched."

He realised that this old cattle trail, which crossed the cañon below him, would scarcely slow up the two riders on that side. There was only one thing to do, and that was to go straight ahead.

The two riders on the left had already come in view; so he spurred a straight course, which would eventually bring him to his own ranch. His horse was breathing easier now, and there was a decided slope.

And Bud was well mounted. He rode high in his stirrups, holding his rifle in one hand, while the horse pounded down across the hills, hurdling, tearing through brush, while behind him came the six men, still scattered, but gradually converging, riding every ounce out of the horses to try to catch the flying quarry ahead of them.

Then the posse began to shoot. It is a difficult feat to hit a running target from the back of a running horse, and Bud knew this well enough to feel little alarm. He was just a little more than holding his own in the race, but he had no idea just where he was going to be when the race was over.

His horse pounded over the crest of a hill, where he was forced to swing to the left to avoid a deep washout, caused by a recent cloud-burst. This had delayed him several moments, giving the posse a chance to close the gap. And as they slowed up at the edge of the washout, two of the men dropped from their saddles, sprawled against an outcropping of granite, and began emptying their rifles at Bud, who was racing his horse across the open country.

A bullet flupped past Bud's ear, another struck a rock just in front of his horse, causing it to swerve. The bullets were coming so close that Bud turned his head and looked back. He could see the horses against the sky-line, and realised that the men had dismounted to do their shooting.

"Run 'em off their feet, bronc!" he panted. "We'll give 'em a trail to foller now."

He leaned forward patting the surging shoulder of his running horse, when something thudded against his leg, and he realised that one of the bullets had found its billet.

CHAPTER XVIII

The sun was nearly down when Hashknife and Sleepy rode in at the ranch again and found Mrs. Daley and Dinah Blewette there. Dinah had driven her down there in the buckboard after some clothes she had forgotten to take with her.

Dug Breed and his man-hunters had crossed the road just ahead of them, and Mrs. Daley questioned Hashknife as to whether some one had given the sheriff information about Bud's hiding-place. Hashknife assured her that no one seemed to know just where Bud was located, but that Breed was making the search on general principles.

She seemed to gather a certain amount of satisfaction from this, but she knew that evading the posse would only make him safe for the time being. Dinah took no part in the conversation; being content to nod or shake his head.

Mrs. Daley gathered up what articles she desired and was putting them into a battered telescope valise, when there came the sound of a running horse and a muttered curse, and a man came up the steps. He flung himself into the doorway, leaning heavily against his elbow, swinging a six-shooter in his right hand.

It was Bud Daley, unkempt, unshaven; his face drawn and haggard. Hashknife had taken a step toward him, but Bud's levelled gun caused him to stop quickly.

"Bud, don't yuh know me?" asked Hashknife.

Bud stared at him, licking his dry lips.

"Good Lord! Hashknife Hartley!" Bud's voice was a croak. "And Sleepy Stevens! Where did you come from?"

His gun-hand waved and dropped to his side weakly.

"Bud, you've been hit, ain't yuh?" Hashknife crossed quickly to him, as Bud lurched forward.

"In the leg," breathed Bud. "The posse is close behind me."

Sleepy quickly closed the door behind Bud, who sank down in a chair. May, her face white with fear, threw an arm around Bud's shoulder and began crying.

Hashknife ran to a window and scanned the hills, which were already dimming in the fading light.

"How far behind yuh is that posse, Bud?" he asked.

"Close," panted Bud. "I think they knew I was headin' home."

"Where did they hit yuh?" queried Sleepy. "In the leg?"

"Yeah. Through my thigh, I think. It's bleedin' quite a lot. They've got me, I guess. I had a rifle; but it wouldn't do me no good to kill 'em. Can't kill everybody, yuh know. Ha-ha-ha!"

Bud laughed from sheer weakness, but there was no mirth in it.

"Don't, Buddie," begged his wife. "Don't laugh like that. We'll take you to a doctor."

"And from there to the pen," said Bud wearily. "Anyway, it's better than dodgin' in the hills. It's a losin' game. But, Hashknife, where did you fellers come from? I can't believe it's you two."

"It's us all right," said Hashknife, his face glued to the window-pane.

The posse had come out on the sky-line of a hill, about five hundred yards away, and were bunched as they debated.

Just away from the front porch stood Bud's horse, one foot on the dragging reins, its head down as it panted wearily from its long run. The buggy team was tied near the back of the house, out of sight of the sheriff and posse.

Hashknife turned from the window. Sleepy

had cut away part of Bud's overall clad leg and was trying to stop the flow of blood. Hashknife examined it quickly and slapped Bud on the shoulder.

"It went plumb through, Bud. You don't need a doctor; we'll fix it up ourselves."

"There ain't much use," said Bud slowly. "They've got me cold. But I'm sure glad to see you two boys. How long have yuh been here, Hashknife?"

"Never mind details, Bud. Sleepy, watch that window."

May Daley came to Bud and took him by the arm.

"Buddy, why won't you talk to me?" she asked tearfully.

Bud gritted his teeth when Hashknife drew the bandage tight, but did not answer her.

"They're scared of yuh, Bud," chuckled Sleepy from the window. "They're still up there on the skyline talkin' it over. They're just a little timid of comin' down."

"They'll come all right," gritted Bud. "If this leg will hold me up for a while, I'll make 'em sorry."

"Stay with it, pardner," grinned Hashknife, getting to his feet and putting a hand on Bud's shoulder. "Tell me the whole truth, Bud. Did you do that job?"

"I did not, Hashknife."

"Good boy! Now, everybody let me alone and we'll see if Dug Breed and his posse are real smart."

CHAPTER XIX

Dug Breed was highly elated, but still cautious. He knew that Bud was in that house, but getting him out might be a different matter; hence the deliberation on the hill top.

"He's hit, I tell yuh," insisted Charley Morse, "I could tell by the way he was ridin' – one foot out of his stirrup."

"That's right," admitted Breed. "He's plugged; but that makes him a bad *hombre* to drag out of a hole. If he wasn't hurt I don't think he'd hole up at home. Kinda funny he didn't shoot back at us, though."

"Nothin' funny about that," snorted Monte. "Bud ain't no danged fool, Dug. He knows too much to waste ammunition on flyin' targets. From now on he'll shoot – and he's a good shot, too."

Breed nodded as he squinted at the house below them. Then:

"We'll surround the place. Monte, you and Caldwell swing to the left and work into that old washout over there; Frank can watch the front, while me and Charley and Brent can swing to the right and work in back of the barn and corrals."

"You've overlooked another bet," said Brent Allard quickly. "There's Hartley and Stevens to look out for."

Breed squinted at Allard and back at the house.

"Do yuh think they'd back Bud's play?"

"You'd be a damn fool to take a chance on 'em not doin' it. I'd rather be safe than sorry."

"Uh-huh." Breed deliberated, but shook his head stubbornly.

"We'll go ahead with our programme. Better move fast, 'cause a movin' object is harder to hit. Let's go."

Swiftly they separated and began their encircling movement. Frank Asher rode straight down the hill with the intention of reaching a thicket of greasewood about three hundred yards from the house, but he had only gone a short distance when he drew his gun and sent two shots into the air.

A man had run from the front door of the ranch-house – a man who limped badly. He

209

caught the horse and mounted slowly. Breed had heard the shots and drew rein, swinging up his rifle. His horse lunged badly on the steep side-hill, making it impossible for him to draw a bead; so he dismounted and began shooting.

But the rider was wasting no time in seeing where the shots were coming from. He swung his horse around the corner of the house, galloped straight across the open ranch-house yard, hurdled the fence and bored straight into the hills. The encircling movement had failed.

Breed swore bitterly and mounted again, racing ahead as he stuffed shells into the loading-gate of his rifle. Monte Sells and Mesa Caldwell were riding swiftly along the slope to the left of the ranch-house, while Frank Asher swung wide and followed in the wake of Breed and the other two riders.

And far ahead of them rode the quarry, riding into the dusk of the hills, holding a straight line toward the Crooked Cañon country. Mile after mile reeled away behind them. It was almost dark now. Breed scowled at the fading light as he rowelled his weary horse to greater efforts.

Suddenly he threw up his head and laughed triumphantly. Monte and Caldwell, better mounted than the rest, had caused the rider to swing farther to the right, and Breed had caught a glimpse of him cutting around the side of a cañon, heading toward the bottom.

"Got him, by gawd!" swore Breed.

He yelled shrilly at Morse and Brent Allard and waved at Frank Asher. Swiftly they gathered around him, their horses blowing heavily.

"We've got him, boys!" panted Breed. "He's headed into that blind cañon just ahead of us. All we've got to do is to smoke him out. C'mon."

"Bud wouldn't head into a blind cañon," protested Allard.

"Well, he did," said Breed laughing. "He didn't know that I had seen him, and he thinks that's the last place we'd ever look for him."

A blind cañon is one of those freaks of nature; like an alley which ends in a blank wall. Usually the sides are precipitous, as is the end. Even the wild things shun them as they would a trap.

The entrance to this one looked harmless enough, sloping away gently to the bottom; but farther along the sides reared higher and higher, impossible of foot-hold. Monte and Caldwell came in from the opposite side and the whole posse met at the mouth of the trap, where they stopped to rest their horses.

"He can't get away," declared Monte, staring into the gloom of the cañon. "I've been in there, and I know that you'd have to have wings to get out. But how did Bud happen to run in there? He knows this place as well as we do."

Breed laughed and dismounted to tighten his cinch.

"That's where he tried to outsmart us, Monte. He figured that we'd never look for him here. It was lucky that I seen him headin' down here. We'll move in to where the sides break straight up and bottle him up. It would be dangerous to move in on him in the dark. He's hurt, I think; and a night up there won't make him any more active than the law allows."

Breed swung back on his horse and they moved ahead. Suddenly they stopped. A rider was coming slowly out of the narrow neck of the cañon. Breed threw up his rifle, but the rider did not pay any attention to it. He was looking up at the sides of the cañon. Then he moved in closer; close enough for them to see that it was Hashknife Hartley.

Breed swore hollowly and lowered his gun. Allard laughed nervously, a chuckling laugh

212

of vindication. Hashknife rode up to them, his face serious, as he motioned back toward the far end of the cañon.

"Say," he remarked easily, "that darn cañon's blind."

"Huh!" Breed crowded the disgust of his soul into one grunt. The rest of the posse merely nodded.

"Yessir, it's blind," continued Hashknife. "A feller could never get out that way."

Then he seemed to consider the posse for the first time.

"You fellers goin' in that way? Don't do it."

Breed spluttered angrily for several moments before his tongue finally shaped words.

"Say, what in hell do yuh think you're doin'? You – huh!"

"Me?" queried Hashknife innocently. "Whatcha mean?"

"You know damn well what I meant! I've got a good notion to arrest you."

"Yeah?" Hashknife seemed amused. "Why don'tcha, Breed?"

Breed looked around at his posse as if trying to seek an answer, but he found them grinning foolishly. Brent Allard seemed almost convulsed with mirth, and it angered Breed.

"What the hell tickles you so darn much, Allard?"

"Well," laughed Allard, "I told you you'd be a blame fool to overlook Hartley."

"Yeah!" Breed snorted and looked back at Hartley, who was grinning softly and offering his sack of tobacco to Monte.

"I reckon we better call it a day," observed Caldwell. "I know I've had all the exercise I need, and my horse twisted two shoes off on that scab-rock below here."

Breed swung his horse around and led them back out of the cañon to the open hills, where he stopped and faced Hashknife.

"Hartley," he said, "I won't forget this. You made a monkey out of me and my posse."

"I'm sorry," said Hashknife soberly. "I didn't mean for yuh to ever catch me; but that danged cañon ruined it."

"How about goin' back to the ranch," suggested Morse.

"Not my gang," said Monte firmly. "If Bud stayed there while we ran the heads off our broncs, he ain't there now."

"Stevens would see that Bud was taken care of," laughed Allard.

"All right!" snapped Breed. "It's too late to do anythin' to-night, anyway."

He swung his horse to the left and they
214

headed across the dusky hills toward Modoc town, while Hashknife rode alone down the hills toward the Triangle-D, grinning into the night.

CHAPTER XX

That same evening Cleve Lavelle stood near one of his roulette tables, which was losing heavily. His face was as expressionless as the face of a savage, but his eyes shifted nervously as the dealer paid out on nearly every turn of the wheel.

He knew that every one was talking about his run of bad luck, and, like a flock of buzzards, they had come to the kill. He turned away from the roulette and walked to a stud game. Mediocre players were bucking the game, and nearly every one of them had an array of red, white, and blue chips in front of them.

Lavelle walked to his private office at the rear and sat down alone, chewing savagely on his cigar. Alone, his features relaxed and he swore softly to himself.

"If this keeps up, I'll be flat broke in a short time," he muttered to himself.

Then he threw his cigar aside and paced the length of the room.

Came a knock on the door, and he wheeled quickly. It was Dug Breed. He squinted at Lavelle and came to the centre of the room, where he leaned on a table.

"Well, what luck?" queried Lavelle uneasily.

It was not often that Dug Breed came to his private office, and he felt that Breed must have a good reason for it now.

And with little omission Breed told Lavelle of running Bud Daley to cover, only to have him escape him. Lavelle listened in silence to the telling, a speculative expression on his face. Then he laughed shortly; an ugly laugh.

"Breed, you are a mighty poor sheriff," he declared.

"All right." Breed shrugged his shoulders. "It was just a case of mistakin' Hartley for Bud Daley, thasall."

"That's all," nodded Lavelle. "You had your chance and missed."

"Didn't miss entirely, Lavelle. Bud was hit."

"Oh, yes, I suppose so." Lavelle was sarcastic, and it nettled Breed.

"Well, it was just a case of Hartley bein' smarter than I was," admitted Breed.

216

Lavelle laughed at Breed's admission, but grew serious.

"It's too damn bad you didn't plug him by mistake."

"I was mad enough to plug him on purpose, Lavelle."

"Well, what are you going to do next, Breed?"

"Search me. I'm goin' to watch Hartley and Stevens for one thing. They know where Bud is, and sooner or later they'll lead me to him. Next time I won't be fooled."

"You better not," said Lavelle coldly. "You make another mistake like that, and you'll not be the next sheriff of Modoc."

Breed lifted his eyebrows slightly and backed slowly to the door, where he stood and looked intently at Lavelle.

"Well, what are you waiting for?" demanded Lavelle.

"I was just thinkin'," said Breed slowly. "They say that you've lost your luck, and I was wonderin' if it would affect you politically."

Lavelle came toward him, a scowl on his face.

"What do you mean, Breed?" he snarled.

"It takes money to run politics – even in a county as small in population as this, Lavelle."

217

"Don't let that bother you, Breed. I'll be leading the parade next election, and don't you forget it. You can either ride with me or you walk alone. Those cheap gamblers out there are only winning chicken-feed."

"Yeah – all right." Breed turned and opened the door. "I'll see how things go, Lavelle."

"Just a moment," said Lavelle, coming closer. "If you need any help, my boys will be free to ride with you."

"And a hell of a lot of good they'll do me!" snorted Breed. "When Hartley laughed at me they laughed with him. *Adios.*"

Breed slammed the door shut, leaving Lavelle staring after him. Then Lavelle went back to the table and selected a fresh cigar from a box. For a long time he chewed on the unlighted weed, his face drawn in a heavy frown.

"Breaking me, are they?" he muttered. "My luck is all gone, eh? I put him in office, but he'd quit me in a minute – the coyote."

Lavelle laughed softly, bitterly, as he crumpled the cigar in his clenched hand. From the gambling room came the sounds of laughter, the rattling of chips, the drone of a dealer's voice. Business was in full sway, and Lavelle knew that the Rest Ye All was losing money every minute.

He went back to the games, where men jostled each other for a chance to place a bet. None of them paid the slightest attention to Lavelle. His games were on the square – no chance for a fixed wheel, a crooked deal – and they knew it. It was just one of those unaccountable runs of ill-luck in which every game in the house suffered heavily.

The stud game halted temporarily while the dealer came to Lavelle and drew him aside.

"Every chip in the rack gone," he said softly. "My game is about four thousand in the hole right now. I've paid out about two thousand in cash."

"Fill your rack," said Lavelle shortly, and walked away.

The dealer nodded indifferently and went back to his game. Lavelle went to the roulette and studied the play. Men were going in on dollar bets and coming away with a hatful of coins.

He walked over to a draw-poker table and sized up the chips in front of the different players, estimating swiftly. The dealer looked up at him inquiringly, but Lavelle walked away and went to the bar. There was nothing he could do. To close the games would be fatal to his prestige. Men would say he was a quitter. Down deep in his heart he wanted

219

to quit, because he knew that he had lost his luck.

Sody Slavin and Uncle Jimmy Miller came in, but did not play. Lavelle knew that Sody had taken a big roll of money out of the place the night before. Other cowboys came rollicking in and added to the noise and smoke of the place. Lavelle turned to the bartender and beckoned him away from the end of the bar, where he was talking to Sody Slavin.

"If anybody wants to see me, I'll be at my room in the hotel."

The bartender nodded.

"Sure, I'll do that."

As Lavelle turned toward the door he came face to face with Jud Mahley. The Black Wells cowpuncher paid no attention to Lavelle, but slouched up to the bar and ordered a drink of whisky.

Lavelle studied him from the rear, a look of half disgust on his face which he could not conceal. Jud gulped his liquor and turned around as Lavelle moved up closer to him.

"Hallo, Mahley," Lavelle spoke softly.

Mahley's ferret-like eyes shifted quickly around the room as he returned the greeting.

"What do you know?" queried Lavelle.

"Not a darn thing."

"Not a thing, eh?"

Mahley shook his head. A couple of cowboys had come in close to them and ordered their drinks. Mahley moved aside, drawing his slouchy sombrero farther down over his eyes.

"Couple of fellers come out to Black Wells," he said to Lavelle. "They didn't like the liquor very well, so they shot the winder out of the Welcome saloon and smashed the mirror of the back bar. That's all the news."

"Who was they?"

One of the cowboys turned his head and looked at Mahley.

"I dunno."

Mahley turned away as if he did not care to talk about it. The cowboys laughed and went back toward the gambling room. Sody and Uncle Jimmy came toward the bar, laughing over some incident of the gambling, and Sody moved in beside Mahley.

Lavelle knew of the enmity between Sody and Jud Mahley, and tried to flash a signal to Mahley; but the signal was lost upon every one except Sody, who saw the action in the mirror.

Quickly he turned his head and looked at the profile of the bad man from Black Wells. Sody did not believe in arguments. With a sideswipe of his big left hand he caught

221

Mahley a slap full in the nose and mouth.

The sound of the blow could be heard all over the house, but was of such a nature that it did little more than sting and partly daze Mahley. He struck his shoulders against the bar and fairly rebounded, his hat flying over the bar and both hands grasping for a support.

For an instant he seemed incapable of action, but instinct caused him to reach for his holstered gun. Sody grunted with glee, swung his right foot in an arc, catching Mahley's legs just behind the ankles and kicked his feet from under him before his hand had quite gripped the butt of his gun.

The shock of Mahley's downfall shook the Rest Ye All, and also took all the fight out of Mahley. He sat on the floor, goggling around, while Sody swiftly disarmed him and tossed the gun over the bar.

"What's the big idea?" queried Lavelle angrily. "What right –?"

"You backin' this scorpion?" asked Sody, pointing at Mahley.

"No, I'm not. But I don't see –"

"You try and see enough to mind your own business, Lavelle."

Lavelle stepped aside while Mahley got slowly to his feet, looking around as if wondering what had happened to him. Then he got a good look at Sody Slavin, and his face reddened with anger.

"Watcha tryin' to do?" he muttered.

"You've got a lot of nerve to be showin' up around here," said Sody. "If I wasn't tender-hearted I'd unwind you, Mahley. And if you show up here ag'in, I'll jist about do that. Now you git off the Modoc range and stay off, you brand-buster."

Mahley's right hand felt of the empty holster, and his eyes squinted almost shut. He blinked his little eyes angrily and started to say something, but changed his mind.

"You ain't goin' fast enough to suit me," said Sody. "If I was you I'd be half-way to Black Wells by this time."

"Aw right."

Mahley turned toward the door, and Sody stared after him. Mahley appeared to be perfectly willing to leave; but at the door he drew a six-shooter from inside his dirty flannel shirt bosom and whirled on Sody.

"Damn you, I'll show you!" he snarled, half sobbing with wrath, as he threw down on Sody.

But before he could pull the trigger a man dived through the doorway into him, and he went staggering sideways, the bullet tearing along the wall.

The man who had knocked him sidewise

fell to his knees from the rush, leaving Mahley still able to recover for another shot; but another man came through right behind him and was into Mahley with both hands swinging like pistons.

The first man was Hashknife Hartley, the second Sleepy Stevens. Neither man said a word. Hashknife got to his feet in time to see Mahley sway forward and catch one of Sleepy's punches flush on the chin. Then Mr. Mahley of Black Wells folded up like an old shirt and went to sleep. And, without any lost motions, Sleepy picked him up in his arms, staggered to the doorway and threw him bodily into the street.

Sody's altercation with Mahley had drawn quite a crowd, and now they stood open-mouthed and stared at Hashknife and Sleepy. Hashknife dusted off his knees with his hands and grinned slowly. Lavelle had not moved, but now he looked keenly at Hashknife before turning away.

"That was kinda complete," remarked Sody with a sigh of relief. "I'm sure much obliged, gents. You came just in time. Mebbe he ain't a very good shot, but I'm big enough for anybody to hit at that distance."

"You don't need to thank me," grinned Sleepy, blowing on his sore knuckles. "I've been honin' for a crack at that horse hobo.

And I sure got my fill. He rattled like a handful of poker chips when I hit him on the chin, didn't he?"

"Mebbe we better take another look at him," suggested Sody. "You never can tell how many more guns he's got with him."

They filed outside and looked around, but there was no sign of Jud Mahley. In the space of two minutes he had recovered from his knockout and had faded from view.

"And I'll betcha he never even stopped to bother with a horse," laughed Sody. "He knows now that Modoc ain't healthy. Let's all go and have a drink."

They went back to the bar. The curious crowd had gone back to the gambling room, leaving only the bartender to applaud them.

"You sure knocked on his gate," he told Sleepy, grinning. "I ain't never seen anybody nail 'em sweeter."

"Wasn't he talkin' to Lavelle?" asked Sody.

"Yeah, he was," said the bartender. "Most everybody around here knows Jud Mahley. He's kinda tough, I'd say."

"Well, he got softened up quite a little," laughed Sody. "Let's have another little snifter and help break Lavelle. Everybody wins from the house these days."

They all trooped into the gambling room and began laying small bets on the roulette.

225

There was no sign of Lavelle, but there was plenty of talk about the ill-luck of the house. Neither Hashknife nor Sleepy felt inclined to gamble heavily, but preferred to stand by and watch the others buck the games.

Uncle Jimmy tried to get Sody to break away and go home; but the fat cowboy was adding to his bank-roll and did not want to leave any easy money behind.

Dug Breed left the saloon before Mahley came in; so did not witness Mahley's downfall. He felt sure that Hashknife and Sleepy would stay there a while. Charley Morse was at the office when Breed came in, reading a magazine.

"We're goin' to take a ride, Charley," said Breed. "Hartley and Stevens are at the Rest Ye All, and the games are runnin' high; so they'll probably stay a while.

"I've got a hunch that Bud Daley comes back to his ranch at night, and this is a good time to prove if I'm right."

"Do yuh really think that Bud got hit, Dug?"

"Somethin' went wrong with one leg, Charley. Sometimes I have to laugh when I think of us chasin' Hartley all the way to that blind cañon. He sure fooled us fine. It wouldn't be hard for me to hate that lean-faced puncher – sometimes."

226

"I dunno." Morse shook his head slowly. "Dug, I don't believe Bud Daley is guilty. I was glad it was Hartley instead of Bud. Of course, we've got to catch Bud if we can."

"Yeah, we've got to," nodded Breed. "The law says he's guilty, whether he is or not. But, Charley, there's somethin' that seems to tell me that the men who stuck up that train and turned Bud loose pulled the job for that purpose."

"Yuh mean they held up the train just to turn Bud loose?"

"Yeah. It looks thataway to me."

"Pals of Bud?"

"Nope. Aw, I dunno where I get the idea, Charley – but I do. There's a nigger in the woodpile somewhere. What was Red Blair doin' out at Bud's ranch?"

"And there yuh are," said Morse. "Too darn many questions."

"Yeah," sighed Breed. "Well, we'll saddle up and see what we can see."

They went out to the stable and saddled their horses. No one saw them leave. The fight with Jud Mahley was over, and the games were running full blast. Breed and Morse rode past the Rest Ye All hitch-rack to see that Hashknife and Sleepy's horses were still there, and then headed for Bud's ranch.

A faint moon illuminated the Modoc hills.

227

The sounds of Modoc revelry faded out behind them, and they rode through a silent world, with only the soft plop, plop, plop of their horses' hoofs in the dusty road which stretched ahead like a faint ribbon in the moonlight.

"Man-hunters," said Morse softly. "Goin' out to try and catch a man on a night like this. Wantin' to send him to a prison, cuttin' him off from everybody, everythin' – moonlight, the hills, everybody. Dug, I hate this kinda work."

"I don't like it, Charley. I'd like to have Bud ridin' along with us here, goin' out to the ranch. But I suppose somebody has to do the job. This kind of a night gets into my blood, and I – I dunno."

Breed shook himself in his saddle, shifting back and forth.

"My cinch is loose," he said. "This blamed bronc blows himself full of wind when I tighten the cinch. Whoa!"

He swung down and lifted his saddle-fender preparatory to tightening the cinch. Morse drifted on slowly, and was a few yards beyond the sheriff, when a streak of flame darted up from some brush beside the road beyond him, followed by the thudding report of a shotgun.

The sheriff sprang back, clawing at his face. It seemed as though some invisible animal had clawed him in the face. He saw Morse's horse whirl and go past him, running madly, but Morse was lying in the middle of the road, a black blot against the yellow dust. Breed staggered ahead, brushing the blood from his eyes, his gun ready, swearing painfully. But there was no more shooting.

He knelt down beside Morse and looked him over. The deputy was dead. Somewhere a night-bird called softly. Breed got to his feet and went back to his horse.

"Who knew we were comin'?" he asked himself. "Who laid for us? They killed poor Charley Morse, who never hurt anybody. This sure is a hell of a finish for him."

He mounted his horse and headed for Modoc.

CHAPTER XXI

Time passes swiftly when stakes are running high, and it was about two hours after the incident with Jud Mahley when Hashknife, Sleepy, and Uncle Jim went back to the bar-room. They had about decided to ride home and were going to take a farewell drink, when Dug Breed staggered through the doorway.

His face was streaked with blood, as if something with many claws had scratched him, and he was dishevelled and covered with dirt. He spat dryly and reached for a glass of whisky which Uncle Jimmy had poured out for his own use. Gulping the liquor at one swallow, he leaned against the bar and swore hoarsely.

"Morse is dead," he croaked, shaking his head painfully. "He never knowed what hit him. I – I –" he felt tenderly of his face, "I reckon I got the drag of the load."

"You sure look like you got somethin'," admitted Hashknife.

"Who killed Morse?" queried Sody wonderingly.

"Gawd only knows. His horse ran away, and mine won't pack double, so I had to leave him there in the road. Somebody bushwhacked us with a shotgun. I was a little behind Charley. Look at my face!"

"Where did it happen?" asked Hashknife.

"Between here and Bud Daley's ranch, just a little beyond where the JM road forks. I couldn't bring Charley in. But he's dead; so it won't matter to him. I've got to find a doctor and take him out there. Luckily it didn't hit me in the eyes."

He turned and staggered outside. The word ran swiftly through the gambling room, and the crowd quit playing to find out the particulars. Some one went to Lavelle's office at the rear and told him what had happened. He added his voice to the rest, and hurried down to the doctor's house to get further particulars from Breed.

No one seemed to be able to figure out just why the sheriff and his deputy should have been ambushed – unless Bud Daley had done it. Hashknife smiled grimly at their conjectures. He knew what had happened or thought he did.

Jud Mahley, smarting over what had happened to him, had secured a shotgun and planted himself beside the road. In the darkness he had mistaken Breed and Morse for Hashknife and Sleepy, never expecting any one except them to ride over that road that night.

And Sleepy had arrived at the same conclusions. He drew Hashknife aside.

"Cowboy, it's a good thing we didn't get there first," he said softly.

Hashknife nodded and they walked outside to their horses.

"Breed and Morse were goin' to the ranch," declared Sleepy. "They knowed we were here; so they thought it might be a good chance to look for Bud."

"And some of them danged fools are

blamin' poor Bud," said Hashknife disgustedly. "We know what happened, but we'll never be able to prove it. Still –" he swung into his saddle – "never is a mighty long time, Sleepy."

The murder of Charley Morse shocked even the sensibilities of Modoc. It was so uncalled for, so fiendish, that those who were hard-bitten enough to overlook an ordinary killing longed for a chance to get their hands on the murderer.

Morse had never been popular, but he had never been unpopular. He was soft-spoken, reliable, minded his own business, and was an efficient officer. The charge of bird-shot had scattered enough merely to rake Breed's features and drill some little holes in his neck and shoulders.

The shooting had been done at fairly close range and, from the extent of Morse's wounds, the assassin had fired both barrels. Hashknife and Sleepy had ridden back to town fairly early in the morning and had a talk with Breed, whose face was plentifully decorated with bits of court-plaster.

Breed was frankly worried. It looked to him as if some one was trying to put the sheriff's office out of commission. But he did not have the slightest idea of who had killed Morse. Only fate had put Morse ahead of him that night. A loose cinch, which he had stopped to tighten, caused him to be riding far enough behind to have escaped the force of the shotgun load.

"You were lookin' for Bud, wasn't yuh?" asked Hashknife.

Breed rubbed his speckled face and nodded slowly.

"Yeah, we was, Hartley. I knowed that you and Stevens were here in town; so we rode out there, intendin' to take a good look at Bud's ranch. You foxed us the other day, but I ain't holdin' no hard feelin's toward yuh.

"Bud and me never did hitch. He's a wild sort of a jigger, and just a kid; but he ain't a feller that yuh can dislike a lot. It ain't me that wants him, Hartley; it's what I represent. The law says he's guilty – not me."

Hashknife held out his hand to Breed, who took it wonderingly.

"Yo're kinda human, Breed," said Hashknife warmly. "Mebbe I've misunderstood yuh all the time. Let's set down and have a talk."

Hashknife indicated a spot on the board sidewalk and they sat down together, where no one would overhear them.

"You don't think that Bud Daley killed Morse, do yuh?" queried Hashknife.

Breed shook his head quickly.

233

"No, I don't, Hartley. Bud Daley ain't that kind. Bud would shoot if he had to, but not from ambush with a shotgun."

Hashknife glanced across the street. Uncle Jimmy and Ma Miller had driven in and were tying their team to a hitch-rack. The hitch-racks were filling up fast. Hashknife grinned and turned to Breed.

"Saturday is always the same in all ranch countries," he observed. "Everybody comes in to trade and tell lies. If it wasn't for Saturday, I'd live in a city."

Breed grinned and nodded. Lavelle came out of the Rest Ye All, spoke to Uncle Jimmy and Ma for several moments and walked down the street. Hashknife watched him keenly and turned to Breed.

"Funny about Lavelle's luck, ain't it, Breed?"

Breed glanced after Lavelle and nodded slowly, a slight frown on his face.

"Do you believe in luck, Hartley?"

"Yeah." Hashknife nodded slowly. "I believe in it, sheriff; but not the way Lavelle does. He's superstitious; believes in signs and charms, I hear."

"Yeah, he does." Breed laughed shortly. "Most gamblers do."

"They're poor sticks to tie to," declared Hashknife. Breed looked up quickly.

234

"What do yuh mean, Hartley?"

"Lavelle got you into the sheriff's office, didn't he?"

Breed's face flushed hotly, but he shut his lips tight.

"He thinks the office belongs to him," continued Hashknife easily. "I know how you feel about it." Hashknife dug his heel into the dirt and squinted thoughtfully, as he said,—

"Breed, did you ever wonder what became of Bud's cattle?"

"Yeah; but I never figured it out. Bud could 'a' bunched 'em and taken 'em to Black Wells. Lavelle thinks that Bud done it. Yuh see, Bud owes Lavelle five thousand dollars, and Lavelle thinks that Bud sold his cattle and lied about 'em bein' stole; so he won't have to pay it back."

"And who do yuh think them two men were that took Bud away from you that night on the train?"

Breed shut his lips tight and shook his head. Lavelle was riding up the street from the livery-stable. He had changed to boots and chaps, and sat his horse as easily as any cowpuncher in the country. He nodded to Hashknife and Breed as he passed them and rode out of town.

"I don't know who them two men were," said Breed thoughtfully. "But it strikes me

235

that the hold-up was just a blind to stop the train and release Bud."

Hashknife laughed and began rolling a cigarette. Breed looked curiously at him and said,—

"Does it strike you as funny?"

"It's so danged mixed up, Breed. If it was only a blind, why did they dynamite that safe in the express car? Their intentions were good, don'tcha think?"

"I dunno. Still, it looks like it might 'a' been just – well, I dunno whatcha call it. I can't imagine who the robbers were."

Breed shook his head seriously, but turned to Hashknife with a grin.

"That jasper that made me unlock Bud's handcuffs was a queer jigger. When he found that you didn't have any money, he gave yuh some."

"Cold-blooded bluff," said Hashknife grinning. "Gentleman bandit stuff. Wanted to show that he was plumb salty, thasall. Well, we don't know much, do we, Breed? Now let's talk about the bank robbery.

"That happened late at night. Somebody knowed that the cashier was workin' late; so he must 'a' waited for the cashier to come out of the door. Then he jist about shoved a gun in his ribs and hurried him back inside.

"Mebbe he made the cashier open the vault. Then he pops the cashier over the head with his gun. He thinks that the cashier is cool for a spell; so he proceeds to loot the vault. About that time the cashier wakes up and makes a break for the door.

"This robber gent takes a shot at the cashier, misses him, busts the window and kills Sody's bronc. The next shot gets the cashier dead centre. Then this man takes his plunder and makes a getaway. Ain't that about the ticket?"

"That's the way I see it," nodded Breed. "I found a rosette off Bud's chaps on the vault floor, kinda mingled with some loose money. I'd know that rosette anywhere. At daylight I beat it for the ranch and found Bud jist pullin' in. He'd sure been ridin' a lot that night, and he won't tell where. His wife don't know, except that he ain't been home.

"We do know that Bud got kinda drunk that evenin' and said he was goin' home. He was kinda raisin' thunder around here – him and Sody Slavin and Dinah Blewette. Dinah and Short-Horn Adams had a fight and Dinah got licked. Then Sody proceeds to lick Short-Horn – or to fix him so Dinah can lick him – which he does to the queen's taste. But that was long after Bud disappeared."

237

"And Bud needed the money, didn't he?" queried Hashknife.

"Yeah. He tried to borrow more from Lavelle that evenin', but didn't get it. I don't blame Lavelle. Bud wanted me to try and find his cows; but I was convinced that he'd sold the darn things; so I got mad at him for askin' me to hunt for 'em. If Bud shot Charley Morse –"

"He didn't," declared Hashknife. "He couldn't. You fellers shot Bud through the leg and he can't walk."

"Thasso?" Breed rubbed his chin and grinned at Hashknife.

"Yeah, that's so, Breed. That's an alibi for Bud. I know where Bud is right now, but I'm not goin' to tell you."

"I could arrest you for harbourin' a criminal, Hartley."

"Hop to it," laughed Hashknife.

Breed frowned reflectively. He knew that Hashknife would not tell, and somehow he did not blame him. There was something about the tall, sad-faced cowpuncher that made Breed feel willing to tell him everything he knew.

"Hartley," he asked, "are you a detective?"

"No. I've done things that a detective might 'a' done; but never wore a badge. Didja ever notice that my nose is kinda long and sharp on the end. Breed, I was born to stick my nose into other people's business. I can't help it.

"Sleepy Stevens is my pet pessimist. Any old time I gets to feelin' real smart, he's there to hang crape on my soul. I need him. Cattle-ranges get sick, don'tcha know it? Yeah, they do. I reckon the cities get sick, too; but I don't *sabe* their disease. We're jist cowpunchers, Breed – me and Sleepy – but fate has made us a couple of medicine-men of the cow-country."

"Medicine-men?" queried Breed.

"Yeah – medicine-men, thasall."

Breed smiled and got to his feet as he said:

"All right, Hartley; Modoc needs somethin' in that line. I'm jist a sheriff. Nobody ever gave me credit for havin' brains. They're sayin' that I ought to find the men who robbed that train; find the man who killed Findlay, and find Bud Daley. Now I've lost my deputy and got shot in the face with a scatter-gun. I reckon I've got a job on my hands.

"Like the Irishman said – single misfortunes seldom come alone," laughed Hashknife. "You forgot to mention Red Blair."

Breed looked quickly, suspiciously at Hashknife; but the tall cowpuncher was looking at Brent Allard, who was just riding past them, leading toward the hitch-rack beside the post office. Allard waved at them, and Hashknife nodded.

"We'll add Red Blair to the total," said Breed.

Hashknife looked up quickly and nodded.

"One more won't hurt."

Breed crossed toward the Rest Ye All, and Hashknife turned and sauntered down toward the post office, where Brent Allard was trying to tie a half-broken broncho to the rack. It was a mean-looking glass-eyed gray with a snaky head and ears that seemed to be pinned down.

Allard had passed inside the post office. Hashknife leaned against the corner and studied the animal. In a few minutes Allard came out with a bundle of mail under his arm. He grinned at Hashknife as he stuffed the mail into his coat pockets.

"I seen yuh talkin' with the sheriff," he grinned. "By grab, I didn't think he'd ever speak to yuh after the way yuh fooled him in the blind cañon."

"Aw, we're good friends," laughed Hashknife.

"Uh-huh," Allard glanced toward the saloon and back at Hashknife. "Well, he's got a little sense, anyway."

"That's a plumb forked-lookin' bronc yo're ridin'," observed Hashknife.

"That thing?" Allard's voice was filled with contempt. "Forked? Say," Allard laughed, "that damn bunch of coiled springs never knows when to quit bouncin'. It's about seven miles from here to the ranch, I reckon. Well, that bronc jist went seven miles high. Mebbe it went a little higher than it did long, 'cause there was times that we stuck to the same landin' spot for quite a spell."

"That's a heck of a thing to ride in after mail," laughed Hashknife.

Allard laughed and shoved the animal away from the rack, so he could untie the rope.

"That's what Monte said. But I told him there was so darn much bushwhackin' goin' on these days that I wanted to ride somethin' that would be awful hard to hit – even with a shotgun."

"Is Lavelle out at the ranch, Allard?"

"Naw. He don't come out much. Well, I've got to git ready to hammer this jug-head out of town."

The gray whirled wickedly, but Allard cramped its head back against its shoulder and snapped into the saddle. For a moment there was a blur of whirling horse and man; then the horse went high in a lunging pitch that almost unseated Allard, and

241

sent a shower of mail from both his coat pockets.

Swiftly the gray changed ends, its head seemingly locked between its front feet, but Allard stuck like a burr. Into the street they went and the gray broke into a run, which took them out of town, like the fading of a motion picture on the screen.

Hashknife gathered up the mail from the dust and started into the post office, but a glance at one of the dusty envelopes caused him to flash a quick glance around as he swiftly slid it inside his shirt.

He walked into the post office and told the postmaster what had happened.

"I'll put it back," grinned the old man, "I don't reckon it's perishable. Ha-ha-ha-ha!"

Hashknife laughed with the old man and went outside. Sleepy and Sody had seen the bucking horse, and now they came across the street. They had imbibed several drinks and insisted on Hashknife joining them, but Hashknife was not in the mood.

Uncle Jimmy and Ma Miller came out of a store, and Hashknife got rid of Sleepy and Sody by hailing them.

"C'mon, Sleepy," urged Sody. "If Ma smells liquor on me, she'll gimme hell. She always tells me a story about a feller who got all stunted to nothin' from whisky.

Pers'nally, I ain't scared of not growin' any more. C'mon."

Hashknife joined the old folks and asked where Mrs. Daley was.

"Oh, May stayed home," explained Ma. "She didn't have nothin' to buy, and she naturally don't like to talk to folks. She kinda feels that they're sayin' things about her. You know how it'd be."

"That – and other reasons," grinned Uncle Jimmy.

Hashknife nodded.

"You try and don't talk too much," warned Ma.

"I ain't said nothin', have I?" demanded Uncle Jimmy.

"Then don't repeat it," said Ma, and then to Hashknife:

"Are yuh comin' out soon? Come out and eat, can'tcha. My gosh, you'll ruin yore stummicks eatin' city food down here."

"We'll be out real soon," declared Hashknife. "Mebbe we'll be out to-night."

"You just do that," urged Ma. "I'll set two extra places."

Hashknife laughed and went over to the hitch-rack. Sody and Sleepy had disappeared. Hashknife hesitated for several minutes, but decided to let Sleepy go ahead and have a good time. He mounted his horse and rode out of town toward the ranch.

CHAPTER XXII

Lavelle also knew that Mrs. Daley had been left at the JM ranch. It was the first time since Bud's arrest that Lavelle had had a chance to see her alone, and he lost no time in taking advantage of it.

He was careful to study the ranch-house at a distance before riding in, as he wanted to be sure that no one else was there. He dismounted at the front porch and knocked loudly on the door, but there was no response. He tried the door and found it unlocked.

Cautiously he opened it. The living-room was empty. Some one was moving about behind the half-open door of an adjoining room. He listened closely, thinking that perhaps his knock had not been heard.

"Hallo," he said softly. "Anybody home?"

There was no reply, but the person in the next room continued to move about. Suddenly the door opened. Lavelle took a step backward, an unspoken exclamation on his lips.

Bud Daley was standing in the doorway, a half-dressed Bud Daley, whose face was flushed with fever, his eyes bloodshot. He blinked at Lavelle, but without a sign of recognition, muttering something unintelligible.

Some one was coming to the front of the house. Lavelle wanted to turn his head, but there was something that caused him to keep his eyes on Bud. Then Hashknife Hartley's voice drawled, –

"Mister Lavelle, meet Mister Daley."

Lavelle turned his head and looked at Hashknife, who was leaning against the side of the doorway. Bud was paying no attention to either of them; he was too sick for that.

"I – I just came," said Lavelle lamely.

"I know yuh did," said Hashknife indifferently, and started to cross the room, when Mrs. Daley came in from the dining-room.

She was dressed for riding. At sight of them she stopped, with a quick intake of breath.

"It's all right," assured Hashknife softly. "There's nothin' to get scared about, May."

"I – I was just going to town after the doctor," she said wearily. "Bud's fever got worse, and there wasn't anybody here to help me."

Hashknife crossed to Bud and took him by

245

the arm. Bud half smiled, as if he recognised Hashknife, but did not speak.

"You get back into bed, old-timer," ordered Hashknife. "You've got to take it easy, don'tcha know it?"

Hashknife assisted him back to bed, where Bud dropped wearily. Lavelle and May were left alone in the living-room, but neither of them spoke. Hashknife was back in a minute and went straight to Lavelle.

"You tryin' to collect that three thousand reward, Lavelle?" he asked.

Lavelle flushed hotly and wished that this long-faced, keen-eyed cowpuncher was miles away. Lavelle had the feeling that Hashknife wanted to make him angry; and Lavelle was too clever a gambler to show his anger.

"The reward does not interest me," he replied. "I just dropped in. But I had no idea that Bud was here."

"You waited until yuh knew that nobody but Mrs. Daley was here, yuh know," reminded Hashknife.

"All right," laughed Lavelle easily. "You did, too."

Hashknife's face grew serious as he nodded slowly.

"Yeah, that's true," he said softly. "I knowed that she was alone – with Bud. Yuh see, I think a lot of these folks, Lavelle. Now, there ain't nothin' for you to do, except to tell the sheriff where Bud is – and collect the reward."

"Damn the reward!" snapped Lavelle. "I'm not looking for any reward."

"No? Well, that's funny," Hashknife laughed shortly. "You let Breed use yore cowpunchers to try and catch Bud."

"He swore them in, Hartley. I couldn't stop him, could I?"

"We've got to get a doctor for Bud," interrupted Mrs. Daley. "All this talk is a waste of time. You stay here and I'll go."

"And the sheriff will find it out," declared Lavelle.

"Will he?" queried Hashknife. "Listen to me, Lavelle. You've got enough power to keep Breed from doin' anythin'. Suppose you go after the doctor? He won't tell. And if Breed finds it out, a word from you will stop him from makin' any arrest."

Lavelle nodded quickly and turned to the door. He was willing to get away. Hashknife followed him out on to the porch and watched him mount.

"Just to save arguments, you might not tell the doctor who the sick person is, Lavelle," he said. "Tell him it's mostly a fever."

"All right," grunted Lavelle.

"And the sheriff won't come out here?"

"I'll do my best," said Lavelle.

"That won't be quite enough," said Hashknife meaningly.

Lavelle glanced keenly at Hashknife.

"Just what do you mean by that?" he asked.

Hashknife's eyebrows lifted slightly and he rubbed his fingers on the nose of Lavelle's horse.

"Yuh understood me, Lavelle," he said slowly. "Doin' yore best would mean that yuh could afford to make a mistake. We don't want any mistakes made in this case.

"You send the doctor out here to attend a sick man; *sabe?* The sheriff don't need to know anythin' about it."

"I see." Lavelle smiled sourly. "You have the mistaken idea that I can run this country to suit myself."

"You won't be runnin' it to suit yourself, Lavelle."

"To suit you – if you like that better."

"To favour humanity," corrected Hashknife.

"All right. But suppose the sheriff finds it out? I can't afford to be charged with compounding a felony. If the doctor chooses, he can notify the sheriff."

"We'll leave that to the doctor, Lavelle. Personally, I don't think Bud Daley is guilty of anythin' worse than bein' a darn fool."

"You don't, eh? The jury thought he was."

"Sure. Well, lots of times twelve men can be bigger fools than one. You just send the doctor out and – thank yuh."

Lavelle turned and rode swiftly away, while Hashknife went back into the house. Mrs. Daley was standing beside Bud's bed, looking down at him, when Hashknife came back in. Bud was mumbling in his delirium a meaningless jumble of broken sentences.

"– price of two dresses," he muttered. "– prettiest woman in this country."

Hashknife glanced keenly at Mrs. Daley. Her lips were shut tightly, and her hands clenched.

"What's he talkin' about?" queried Hashknife.

"– throw away your youth?" queried Bud. "– retain your beauty? Two can't live on cowpuncher's – failure – throw away your life."

Bud laughed bitterly in his delirium. "– silks and furs. Bud is man enough – loyalty and all that."

Mrs. Daley turned away with tears running down her cheeks. Now she knew that Bud had come home and overheard Lavelle and her talking that night. That was why he did not come home; why he did not care what they did to him at that trial. He was willing to go to prison. And this was why Bud would not speak to her.

She walked out into the living-room and sat down in a chair, while Hashknife followed her to the doorway. Bud had quit talking now. Mrs. Daley looked up at Hashknife and found him staring intently at her. "Oh, he's so sick." Her voice sounded strained, unreal, and she knew that Hashknife did not believe that she was overcome on account of Bud's condition.

"What did he mean?" asked Hashknife.

Mrs. Daley turned away, trying to ignore the question; but Hashknife was not to be denied. He came over and put his hand on her shoulder, shaking her a little.

"What did he mean?" he repeated. "Tell me, May."

She looked up at him and tried to get to her feet, but he held her firmly.

"Why, he – he's just delirious," she faltered. "He doesn't know what –"

"It's back in his mind," said Hashknife firmly. "He don't realise what he's sayin', thasall."

"Will Lavelle send the doctor out?" asked Mrs. Daley.

"That's up to Lavelle, May. Now, will yuh tell me what Bud means?"

"I – I don't know, Hashknife."

"You don't need to lie to me, May."

She looked up at him, her lips shut tightly; and she turned away from the determined expression in his eyes.

"And you know yuh lie, when yuh say yuh don't know, May," he said softly. "I'm yore friend – and I'm listenin' real close."

"You – you call me a liar?" she faltered. "And you say you are my friend?"

"I've had a lot of friends that lied, May. That's one of the failin's of the human race. There'll always be liars. Now come clean with me. I want to help yuh, but I've got to have the truth."

She got up from her chair and walked to the front doorway. He followed her and she went out on the porch, where she leaned against one of the porch posts, staring off across the hills. Hashknife leaned easily against the side of the doorway and rolled a smoke. Back in the bedroom Bud muttered some broken sentences.

"Oh, I wish that doctor would hurry," said May nervously.

"It's quite a ways to town," said Hashknife. "But that's all right; Bud ain't in dangerous shape. Are yuh ready to talk?"

"Talk?" She turned on him warily. "Oh, why don't you go away and let me alone? I have nothing to talk about."

He stepped out and put a hand on each of her shoulders, forcing her to look into his face.

"May," he asked softly, "are you in love with Lavelle?"

She shut her eyes quickly and shook her head violently.

"Is he in love with you?"

Quickly she turned away from him, but did not answer.

"All right, I reckon that's it," said Hashknife sadly. "I don't blame him. Yo're a lovable sort of a girl, May. I used to wonder how Bud Daley got yuh." He laughed softly and rubbed his chin.

"Yo're too good for Bud Daley."

She turned quickly, angrily.

"What do you mean by that?" she demanded.

"He's just a cowpuncher, May. You ought to have silks and furs and all that, don'tcha know it?"

Her tightly shut lips trembled and tears came to her eyes. He was goading her with Bud's own words.

"Lavelle could give yuh all them things, May. He told yuh he could, didn't he?"

252

"Oh, why do you ask me these things?" she cried. "What good can it do you?"

"And Bud heard yuh talkin' with Lavelle, didn't he? He heard Lavelle offer yuh all these things, May? When did he hear this?"

"What good –?" she began.

"Was it the night that the bank was robbed?"

She tried to turn away, but he caught her by the arm and their eyes met. She nodded quickly and looked away.

"Thank yuh, May," he said softly. "Now, let's talk about it."

"Oh, I don't want to talk about anything, Hashknife. Please don't ask me to talk about it. I've had so much trouble –"

"Yo're goin' to talk to me," laughed Hashknife, "or I'm goin' to take you across my lap and spank yuh good; *sabe?*"

She turned angrily on him, but her sense of humour saved Hashknife. In spite of herself she was forced to laugh at his threat.

"Right down here on the steps," grinned Hashknife. "We'll set down and have a real good talk. I'm a danged good spanker, too."

They sat down together. It seemed easier to talk now.

"Now," said Hashknife, "I understand that Lavelle loves you, but you don't love him. Makes it tough on Lavelle, but lucky for you.

253

And the night of the bank robbery Bud heard Lavelle makin' love to you, eh?"

"I didn't know it," she confessed. "But those were some of the things that Lavelle said to me; so Bud must have overheard."

"Prob'ly broke Bud all up. He had tried to borrow more money from Lavelle that day. Makes it look bad for Bud. He needed money to buy yuh the things that Lavelle promised yuh. It's a good thing yuh didn't have to testify at the trial, or they'd 'a' hung him on that kind of testimony.

"Would you – say, May, this is gettin' danged personal, and mebbe yuh won't answer it, but I'm asking it just the same: if Bud had gone to the penitentiary, would you have married Lavelle?"

"I don't love Lavelle," she replied softly.

"He wanted to marry yuh, didn't he?"

"Yes – for a long time."

"Uh-huh. And if Bud was sent to the penitentiary you could marry him if yuh wanted to, May. There wasn't nothin' to stop yuh."

"I realise that," she said slowly. "Lavelle offered to take me away from here – away from Modoc. He said he would sell out and we could see the world. He came to me again, after Bud was convicted. But I told him that it was impossible. I was so sick over it all.

He begged me to go away with him, but I refused. I told him that I was Bud's wife as long as he lived – no matter what he had done."

"That was square of yuh, May," said Hashknife softly. "I'm kinda proud of yuh, don'tcha know it?"

"And you don't blame me, Hashknife?" she asked eagerly.

"Not that I know of," he smiled. "It wasn't no fault of yours, if Lavelle loved yuh. You wouldn't be hard to love. If I was ten years younger I'd love yuh myself."

She laughed softly and the colour came back to her face.

"I didn't know that age was a barrier to love," she said.

"There's different kinds of love, May. The kind you know is yore love for Bud. That's the love of youth. If I was ten years younger –" Hashknife laughed and got to his feet. "Gettin' kinda stiff in the knees."

"You are not over forty, Hashknife."

"Well?"

"Lavelle is almost forty."

"And yo're about twenty-two. Say, you ain't tryin' to make love to me, are yuh, May?"

"Certainly not!"

"Squirshed agin'," said Hashknife

255

dejectedly. "I never did have no luck. I got stuck on a waitress in Cheyenne once. She had the prettiest hair I ever seen. I reckon I got stuck on her hair. Well, one day she was waitin' on my table and I asked her to go to a dance with me that night. I was sure goin' to ask her to marry me that night." Hashknife laughed softly and rubbed his chin.

"Well, she said she'd go with me. She was standin' agin' the wall, where the hooks are that yuh hang yore coats on, and when she turned to go back to the kitchen, her hair got caught on a hook – and stayed there."

"Stayed there?" wondered May.

"Uh-huh." Hashknife laughed heartily. "It was a wig. She was as bald as an aig. She beat it for the kitchen; so I got the wig and gave it to the cashier. That was my only experience as a hair-restorer."

Mrs. Daley laughed heartily over Hashknife's sorrows, and to take her mind off the long wait for the doctor, he told her some of the experiences that he and Sleepy had encountered; telling them in a whimsical way, taking no credit for himself.

It was an hour or so later that the doctor

arrived. He asked no questions, but proceeded to administer to Bud, who had recovered to a certain extent. Uncle Jimmy and Ma Miller came home, excited over the presence of the doctor, until Hashknife explained how it had all happened.

"And what was Lavelle doin' out here?" demanded Ma Miller.

"I reckon he just dropped in," said Hashknife.

"Dropped, eh?" Ma was suspicious and did not conceal it.

"Ma, it's none of yore business," said Uncle Jimmy, glad of a chance to chide her. "He didn't come out here to see you, 'cause he knowed you was in town."

"Yeah, and he knew that May was here alone. I don't like it."

Ma bustled away into the kitchen, and Hashknife went back to his horse. Uncle Jimmy begged him to stay for supper, but Hashknife declined.

"Mebbe t'morrow night. I've got some folks that I want to see pretty soon."

"Well, make it to-morrow night, then," said Uncle Jimmy regretfully. "Ma'll probably raise hell when she finds out that yo're gone, but yo're single and can do as yuh darn please. Might do her good to find out that she can't boss everybody."

CHAPTER XXIII

Hashknife rode back toward town deep in thought. He drew out the letter he had purloined from the 76-A mail and looked it over again. It was directed to Cleve Lavelle and post-marked Black Wells. Inside was a single sheet of paper on which was written in lead pencil:

$75 dols. Plese remit.

It was unsigned. Hashknife grinned as he touched a lighted match to a corner of it and watched it burn to ashes. Then he rode on into Modoc and tied his horse to the Rest Ye All rack.

There were three horses at the rack, which looked as if they might have travelled a long ways. Hashknife noticed that two of them bore a Cross-Arrow, while the third was branded with three parallel bars on the left hip. He had seen these brands at Black Wells. It was evident that some of Black Wells had come to Modoc, and he wondered if it was any of the gang that were in the Welcome saloon when Sleepy had bombarded the place.

Modoc was a well patronised town on Saturday. There were many men in the Rest Ye All, but Hashknife decided not to go in. There was no use of running into trouble, which would probably result if he ran into some folks he knew in Black Wells.

He crossed the street and ran into Breed, who seemed visibly worried. He jerked his thumb in the direction of the hitch-rack at the Rest Ye All.

"Jud Mahley and a couple of other hard roosters came over from Black Wells t'day, Hartley. They're in the saloon drinkin' hard liquor and keepin' an eye on the door. Sleepy and Sody are down at the Elite saloon singin' songs to a bartender who don't care for music."

"Well, he ain't hearin' any," laughed Hashknife.

Breed grinned shortly and squinted the length of the street.

"I know. But there'll be hell to pay if them two meet Mahley and his two friends. I figure that they came here to get even for what happened to Mahley. He's a dirty coyote, Hartley; and the two men with him ain't no better. What had we better do?"

"Well," said Hashknife slowly, "I reckon we better find a preacher and have him pray a few times for Mahley and his two gun-men.

I dunno much about Sody Slavin, but I know that Sleepy is able to protect his own hide."

"I wasn't worryin' about Sody," grinned Breed. "He's a big, fat son of a biscuit-shooter, but he's a humdinger in a fight. You kinda figure in this too, don'tcha?"

"Oh, that don't matter. I'll kinda keep out of sight, I s'pose."

Breed laughed and hitched up his belt. He felt better about it now.

"You ain't worryin', are yuh?" asked Hashknife.

"No-o-o, I reckon it'll be all right. Had supper yet?"

"Nor dinner," grinned Hashknife. "Plumb forgot it. Let's get Sody and Sleepy and all go to eat together. It'll give us a good chance to keep 'em away from Juddie and his gang."

"That's the ticket." Breed was enthusiastic, but became dubious.

"I seen 'em a while ago, and they wasn't open to suggestions. Mebbe you can convince 'em, I dunno."

They found the two cowpunchers in the Elite, leaning against the bar, while Sody was trying to tell Sleepy a story about Christopher Columbus. It dealt with Columbus' feat of standing an egg on end. Sody had the egg. The bartender, a sleek, fat individual, with a scant growth of hair, well plastered down, was interested in the narrative, and none of them paid any attention to the coming of Hashknife and Breed.

"Well, how'd he do it?" asked Sleepy, owl-eyed. "Yuh can't stand no aig on end, Sody. It ain't built thataway, I tell yuh. Old Chris must 'a' had a hen that laid a flat-ended aig."

"Noshir," Sody wagged his head wisely. "Here's how he done it."

Sody grasped the egg firmly in his ham-like hand, held it aloft in triumph.

"Wa'sh me closely," he chuckled. "There's no mushtash to desheeve the eye. Ol' Chris jus' took the aig – thusly, and –"

Thump! Sody brought his hand down hard enough to have broken a much tougher article than an egg, and the contents of the fruit of the hen-house squirted all over the interested bartender.

He backed against the back bar, clawing the yolk out of his eyes, while Sody looked goggle-eyed at the crushed mass in his palm. Sleepy moved back, his nose twitching.

"Didja see her stand on end?" asked Sody foolishly.

"I didn't see it," said Sleepy. "But I betcha it could. My Gawd, that aig was old enough to whip the hen that laid it."

"You've gotta lot of nerve," wailed the

bartender, brushing furiously at the gobby-goo on his white vest. "Next time yuh want to tell stories keep away from here. My gosh, that's a strong egg!"

Sody reached across the bar and dragged the palm of his hand across the edge to dislodge the remnants of the egg, while with the other hand he held his nose.

"Well, 'f here ain't m' fambly!" exclaimed Sleepy, catching sight of Hashknife. "Yo're late, cowboy. Sody jist showed us how to stand an aig on end. C'mon and have a drink."

"You've had a plenty," grinned Hashknife. "You and Sody are invited to eat supper with me and the sheriff."

"We ain't under arrest, are we?" queried Sody quickly.

"Not yet – but the evenin' is still young. C'mon."

"There's somethin' wrong," declared Sleepy wisely. "They want to keep an eye on us, Sody. Whatcha s'pose it is?"

"I dunno, and I don't care," declared Sody. "I'm hungry – but not for aigs. Waugh! A voice from the tomb. C'mon, let's go."

They went up the street to a restaurant and ordered their meals. Sleepy was suspicious. He knew that there was a reason for bringing them up there, and in a few minutes Hashknife told them.

"Great lovely dove!" exploded Sody. "That lop-eared whangdoodle came back here? Mamma mine, what we'll do to him will be a joy for the Cannibal Islands. Where are they, Hashknife?"

"Set still," ordered Hashknife. "You two jiggers are goin' to promise me that yuh won't start no trouble. Until the proper time Mahley and his gang are as safe as a church; *sabe?*"

"Oh, yeah!" snorted Sleepy indignantly. "They came back here to get even with us – and we've got to take it, eh?"

"No, I don't mean that, Sleepy; and you know I don't. Keep away from Mahley and his men. You don't need to butt into 'em, do yuh?"

"It would be a lot of fun," muttered Sleepy. "I want to take a shot at that bat-eared pelican. He ain't no good, dang his hide."

"But yuh won't take no shot at him, Sleepy," said Hashknife. "I told yuh not to, and you mind me real fine."

"All right," Sleepy nodded violently and upset a glass of water with his elbow. "I'll keep my paws off him for yore sake, but if you kill him without givin' me and Sody a chance at him we'll see that Sandy Claws don't come to yore house next Christmas."

They ate their supper and went back to the street. Hashknife noticed that the three Black Wells horses were missing from the hitch-rack, and sighed with relief. He felt sure that Sleepy and Sody would proceed to forget what they had promised – and prove a good alibi later on.

It was growing dark and Breed lighted a lamp. They sat down and smoked for a while, discussing things in general. The talk drifted around to Bud Daley and his troubles.

"They convicted Bud on a silver rosette, didn't they?" asked Hashknife.

"Yeah," nodded Breed. "Didn't yuh ever see it?"

He flung open a drawer of his desk beside Hashknife and took out the rosette, which had been thrown in on top of some pages. Hashknife examined it closely. It was a hand-made thing and very distinctively hammered and engraved.

"There was no argument about the ownership," said Breed, as Hashknife examined it under the light of the lamp.

He had one hand in his pocket, but now he withdrew the hand.

"Funny how a thing like that will convict a man," he mused. "Bud made it with his own hands, hammered it out to suit himself, and the danged thing made an outlaw out of him.

"Well –" he turned and dropped the shining ornament back into the drawer and shoved it shut – "it's the little things in life that do the damage."

"It sure looks thataway," nodded Breed. "But for some reason I ain't worryin' about catchin' Bud. He's worth three thousand to the man that finds him, and I kinda hope he won't be found. Funny thing for a sheriff to say, ain't it?"

Hashknife laughed softly.

"I'm glad yuh feel thataway, Breed. Mebbe you'll be disappointed, but I don't think so."

"Anyway, I'm not huntin' for him, Hartley. I probably won't be the next sheriff of Modoc."

"Keep yore shirt on," grinned Hashknife. "Every body in the country ain't agin' Bud Daley; and yuh might still get a vote or two."

"All right, Medicine-Man," laughed Breed. "We'll wait and see what happens."

They went over to the Rest Ye All and moved about the gambling room. It was a big night and the games were well patronised. Lavelle was there watching the play. He glanced nervously at Hashknife and Breed, and Hashknife noticed a slight pallor about his face.

Lavelle was not a quiet dresser at any time, but to-night he sparkled with sartorial

265

splendour. He nodded shortly as Hashknife and Breed passed him, but Hashknife did not speak. Lavelle looked after the tall cowpuncher, a half sneer on his lips. He noted the big, holstered six-shooter which seemed to cling tightly to Hashknife's thigh, hanging at just the right angle for a quick draw.

He wondered where Sleepy and Sody were. They had been around earlier in the day. Not that he wanted to see them come in. They were too rough, too boisterous to suit Lavelle; but he rather wanted to know where they were and what they were doing.

Hashknife placed a few bets on the roulette and won the majority of them. But he did not care for roulette. It was all luck, when the wheel was honest. Hashknife preferred to match his brains with others at draw or stud poker. But both big games were filled.

He stood around for a while watching the games and talking with the players. Breed suddenly disappeared. Hashknife looked for him, but he was not in the house; so Hashknife took a seat near the wall and proceeded to smoke a cigarette.

It was about fifteen minutes later that Sleepy and Sody came in. They seemed in a hurry and there was little evidence in their actions that they had ever taken a drink. They saw Hashknife and came straight to

266

him, drawing him away from the crowd.

"It's all off with Bud unless we act quick," whispered Sleepy. "That blamed Mahley found out where Bud is and has told the sheriff."

"How did Mahley find out?" queried Hashknife.

"He told Breed that the doctor told him. Breed just left with a livery-rig, but he told me to tell you. Now, we've got to do somethin' real fast, Hashknife."

"What can we do?" queried Hashknife. "The sheriff knows where Bud is, and Bud's too sick to move. We can't fight the sheriff."

"We can go down and kill that damn doctor," said Sody seriously. "Me and Sleepy are gunnin' for Mahley and his two pet skunks as soon as they show up back here."

"Breed took a livery-rig, eh?" mused Hashknife. "He must figure on bringin' Bud back with him. How long has he been gone?"

"About ten minutes," said Sleepy anxiously. "We can still beat him to the JM if we cut the hills."

Hashknife shook his head slowly and squinted back at the windows of the Rest Ye All.

"No, it wouldn't do us any good, boys. Killin' Mahley won't stop Bud's capture.

267

We've just got to let 'em go ahead; and in the meantime, let's go back and see if Lavelle's luck is still good."

Both Sody and Sleepy grumbled over what they were going to do to Jud Mahley and his two companions, but they followed Hashknife into the gambling house.

Lavelle was watching the stud-game, and Hashknife stopped near him. Lavelle glanced quickly at Hashknife, but turned back to the game.

"You ain't playin' much these days, are yuh, Lavelle?" asked Hashknife.

His voice was loud enough for those at the game to hear, and the dealer looked up at Lavelle, who turned quickly to Hashknife.

"Well, what about it?" Lavelle's voice held a trace of annoyance.

"Ain't takin' chances on bad luck," grinned Hashknife.

Lavelle stared intently at the table for several moments, as if trying to make up his mind what to say. One of the players shoved his chips over to the dealer, who stacked them quickly and shoved the correct amount in coin across to the player.

"Looks like easy money," grinned Hashknife.

"Try it!" snapped Lavelle, indicating the vacant chair.

Hashknife laughed softly, but did not accept.

"I was just wonderin' whether it was yore personal hoodoo, or whether the house was just havin' a run of bad luck."

Lavelle shifted uneasily. Some of the players laughed, and it angered Lavelle. He disliked being laughed at. Suddenly he looked at Hashknife, a sneer on his lips.

"What's all this talk about hoodoos, Hartley? If you've got money enough to make it worth while, I'll gamble with you."

"From what I've seen around here, it don't take much," laughed Hashknife. "A dollar runs into hundreds pretty quick."

"I don't gamble with pikers," said Lavelle coldly and turned away.

"Same here," laughed Hashknife. "So there ain't no chance for us to clash."

Lavelle turned and came back to the table. He was mad. At a signal from him, the dealer got up and let Lavelle sit down in his place. Swiftly Lavelle arranged the chips to suit himself, broke open a new deck of cards and looked up at Hashknife.

"I thought I'd bluff yuh into dealin'," grinned Hashknife, sliding into the vacant chair. "You ought to be easy to beat."

The muscles around Lavelle's thin mouth twitched slightly, but he did not reply.

His hands trembled visibly as he shuffled the cards. The other three players seemed amused, and grinned at the circle of spectators. Sody and Sleepy were in that circle; Sody stolid in his interest, Sleepy alert, because he knew that this gambling challenge was not at all like Hashknife.

Hashknife drew out a roll of bills and tossed five of them across to Lavelle.

"Give me twenty blues," he said.

Lavelle accepted the hundred dollars and shoved the small stack of blue chips across the table, each chip worth five dollars.

"Cash mine in, Lavelle," said one of the players. "I can't see clear enough to bet only five-dollar chips."

Lavelle smiled coldly and counted the man's chips. One of the other players shuffled uneasily, but decided to stay. The other grinned and separated his chips into two piles.

"One's velvet," he said. "I'll play close to m' stummick."

Four blue chips decorated the centre of the green-covered table, and Lavelle began the deal. Hashknife did not look at his hole-card. Monte Sells and Brent Allard came in from the bar and stopped to look at the game.

On the second round, both Hashknife and Lavelle received aces, hearts and diamonds.

Hashknife flipped three blue chips to the centre. Lavelle stayed, but the other two dropped out.

"I'll high-spade yuh for ten dollars, Lavelle," challenged Hashknife, but Lavelle ignored him.

The ace of clubs fell to Hashknife, while Lavelle drew a small card. Hashknife bet five blues, but Lavelle dropped.

"Looks easy," grinned Hashknife, raking in the pot. "I'm better off than the boys were who had inside information that the big pay roll was goin' to Dixon that night."

Lavelle's eyes flashed questioningly at Hashknife, but he was stacking his chips carefully and did not look up. Brent Allard shot a swift glance at Monte Sells, and their eyes met.

On the next deal Hashknife passed without looking at his hole-card. Lavelle gave him a curious look, but Hashknife only grinned and said:

"Luck's a funny thing. Now, take Bud Daley, as an example; he's unlucky. Somebody stole all his cows, and there's a lot of folks who don't know yet who stole 'em."

Lavelle scowled heavily as the player at Hashknife's right won the pot and raked it in with a laugh.

"Is this a poker game or a lecture?" growled Lavelle angrily.

Hashknife grinned widely and rested his elbows on the table.

"I like to entertain folks, Lavelle," he said. "Don't mind me; go ahead with the deal."

The onlookers were beginning to enjoy it. Lavelle was noted for his cold, hard nerve, and it amused them to see him so angry that his dealing was jerky. Hashknife peeked at his hole-card and laughed loudly.

"I've got a card in the hole that looks like Jud Mahley," he announced. "Jud Mahley in the hole, Lavelle. Deal ag'in; this is sure gettin' good."

Hashknife seemed to pay no more attention to his hand, but called the bets as the cards dropped. He had two jacks in sight, while Lavelle's hand showed a pair of eights. The other two players quit. Hashknife bet twenty dollars, and after due deliberation, Lavelle conceded the pot to Hashknife, who uncovered his hole card – a deuce of spades.

"Thought I had a knave, didn't yuh, Lavelle? You knowed that Mahley was a knave. Ha-ha-ha-ha! He's a dirty deuce, too."

Lavelle shut his jaw tightly and shuffled the cards in a savage way.

"Leave some of the spots on 'em,"

cautioned Hashknife. "Jist 'cause yo're mad – don't ruin the pretty cards."

After the next hand, the other two players decided that the pace was too hot for them, and dropped out. Lavelle cashed in their chips, leaving himself and Hashknife to a single-handed battle.

"Speakin' of Jud Mahley," said Hashknife seriously. "There's a lot of pickpockets in Black Wells."

He looked around as if challenging somebody to dispute his statement. Sleepy was grinning widely.

"We know it, don't we Hashknife?" he laughed.

"Danged right. Whisky dopers, too. I understand that somebody in Modoc has got to pay seventy dollars damage to the Welcome saloon. That'll take off some of the profit from Bud's cows."

Lavelle had dealt two cards and was waiting for Hashknife to make his bet. Lavelle's eyes looked strained and there were tiny beads of perspiration about his temples. The crowd around the table, with the exception of Sleepy, did not know what it was all about, but they were more interested in Hashknife than they were in the two-handed stud-game.

"That's what happens when yuh lose yore luck," continued Hashknife, tossing some

chips to the centre. "Feller gets to worryin'
about it and snags himself in his own loop.
Bud didn't have bad luck – he had some bad
friends. Now the sheriff has gone after him.
He's sick in bed, with a bullet-hole in his
leg. They'll bring him back pretty soon. You
callin' my last bet, Lavelle?"

Lavelle was staring at the pot, holding the
cards tightly in his hand. He had called
Hashknife's last bet; but now he called it
again. Which showed that Lavelle's mind was
not on the game.

"Yo're of this game, but not in it," laughed
Hashknife. "But yuh might as well leave that
fifteen dollars in the pot, 'cause I'll get it
anyway. You ain't even got poker sense,
Lavelle."

Lavelle flushed hotly and looked around.
The former dealer was at his elbow, and
Lavelle started to get out of his chair.

"Goin' to change dealers, eh?" sneered
Hashknife. "Afraid to trust yore luck any
further, are yuh, Lavelle? Yo're a hell of a
gambler, you are. Why don't yuh git some
buildin' blocks and play behind the bar,
where nobody can see yuh?"

Lavelle snapped back into his chair, his
face white from the sting of Hashknife's
insults.

"You want to play poker?" he snarled
274

angrily. "You game to play a man-sized game of cards? By God, I'll show you some action. Buy enough chips to make it worth while, you mouthy fool!"

Hashknife leaned across the table and laughed into Lavelle's face.

"You can be bluffed, Lavelle. Right now yore heart is yaller from the gall yo're usin' to brace it up."

Hashknife drew out a bill-fold and took out three one-thousand-dollar bills, which he tossed carelessly across to Lavelle. The ring of onlookers crowded in close to look at the money.

"My Lord!" exploded a cowpuncher. "Thousand dollar bills! I didn't know there was that much money in the world."

"They're a safe size," laughed Hashknife. "If yuh stole one, you'd have a hell of a time disposin' of it in this country."

Lavelle squinted at the money closely.

"How big do you want to play this?" he asked.

"Man-size," laughed Hashknife. "You name the amount. I'm in favour of hundred-dollar chips and no limit."

Sleepy moved in a little closer and tossed a cheap bill-fold on to the table in front of Hashknife.

"Here's another the same size," said Sleepy
275

indifferently. "Give him plenty of action, cowboy."

Hashknife grinned up at Sleepy and nodded his thanks. Lavelle flashed a glance at Sleepy, but continued to count out chips. His fingers trembled slightly and a chip fell to the floor as he shoved thirty chips across to Hashknife.

It was the biggest price ever paid for poker chips in Modoc, and it did not take the whole room long to find out that something out of the ordinary was going on at the stud table.

It was out of the ordinary for cowpunchers to have as much money as Hashknife and Sleepy had shown, and many of the onlookers glanced significantly at each other. But the money had been honestly earned. It was their pay for cleaning up a crew of rustlers in the Ghost Hills, which had happened but a short time previous to their arrival in Modoc. Hashknife had insisted on taking the money in thousand-dollar bills, because it would be more difficult for them to get one cashed. Both he and Sleepy had visions of saving enough to buy them a little outfit and go into the cattle business.

CHAPTER XXIV

The crowd grew silent as the game began. Lavelle's face was a set mask under the yellow light of the big lamp. Hashknife's grin hid any emotion he might have felt, and he handled hundred-dollar chips as if they were pennies.

Hand after hand they played, one player or the other conceding the pot, after two or three cards had been dealt. Neither man was winner as yet; but every one knew that sooner or later they would get the cards they were looking for.

"Kinda funny about Charley Morse," observed Hashknife, as he peered at his hole-card. "The feller that killed him didn't have a shotgun until he came to Modoc. Yuh see, he didn't have nothin' agin' Charley Morse nor Breed. He wanted to kill me or my pardner. It was just another fool mistake. Killers all make mistakes."

The crowd was listening intently, wondering. Lavelle shifted in his chair, looking nervously at Hashknife as he said hoarsely, –

"You calling my bet?"

Hashknife rolled two chips to the centre, and they promptly circled and rolled back to his side of the table.

"They know where the luck is," laughed Hashknife. "They want to come back to me, Lavelle."

Lavelle muttered a curse and dealt the next card. The board showed that Hashknife had a jack and a six, while Lavelle had a pair of tens.

"Twenty miles of railroad," laughed Hashknife. "Yore bet."

After a moment of hesitation, Lavelle shoved five hundred dollars to the centre. Hashknife laughed softly and fingered his chips.

"Mahley in the hole," he muttered. "A jack and six in sight. That beats a pair of tens, so I call."

He shoved in five chips and grinned widely. Lavelle studied Hashknife's hand, a half-smile on his lips, as he said:

"Are you playing table-stakes, Hartley?"

Hashknife laughed softly and leaned back in his chair.

"You make your bets, Lavelle. I've got over six thousand here."

Lavelle flipped off the next two cards, which showed another six for Hashknife and a trey for himself. Hashknife's hand showed a pair of sixes and a jack, while Lavelle's showed a pair of tens and a trey.

"Yore tens are still good," grinned Hashknife.

Lavelle shoved five chips to the centre. Hashknife laughed as he shoved in five chips to cover the bet and then added ten more as a raise.

"My gosh!" exploded a cowpuncher. "Raised him a thousand!"

Lavelle moistened his lips with the tip of his tongue and stared hard at Hashknife, who was rolling a cigarette with hands that did not tremble. Again Lavelle looked at the pip on his hole-card. It was a six spot. He realised that there were big odds against Hashknife having a six spot in the hole.

And he remembered that Hashknife had said that he had a "Mahley" in the hole. The last time it had been a deuce; this time it might be a jack. Lavelle's fingers trembled over his chips.

"That bank robbery was a funny deal," said Hashknife, and Lavelle looked up quickly.

"Funny thing that Bud would pick the vault to lose that silver rosette in," continued Hashknife thoughtfully. "It's too bad that the cashier didn't live long enough to tell who done it. He knew, too."

"Oh, for God's sake, shut up!" snarled

279

Lavelle. "What's all the talk about, anyway?"

"I'm tryin' to take yore mind off yore bad luck," laughed Hashknife. "I want yuh to call that thousand; but yo're afraid to do it, when you stop to think. You know where yore luck went, but that don't help yuh any, Lavelle. Yuh get kinda sick in the stummick, when yuh think about it, don'tcha?"

Lavelle's eyes narrowed, as he shoved ten chips into the pot.

"Bluffed yuh into it, eh?" Hashknife laughed triumphantly. "Yuh didn't do that because yo're brave; yuh did it because yo're plumb scared to death."

"What in hell are you talking about?" said Lavelle hoarsely.

"Yore luck. Go ahead and deal."

Lavelle picked up the deck and dealt two more cards. A gasp went up from the crowd, when they saw that Hashknife had drawn another six, while Lavelle had another ten-spot.

Lavelle stared at the two hands and a smile of triumph flashed across his lips.

"What about luck now, Hartley?" he asked nervously.

Hashknife lifted his eyes from an inspection of the two hands and grinned widely.

"Yore three ten bets, Lavelle."

There was no nervousness in Hashknife's

voice – only amusement. Lavelle hesitated. He had faced many a man across the green cloth, but this man was different from the rest. That third ten had brought the courage back into Lavelle's heart, but now he felt it oozing away again.

The crowd moved slightly, and Hashknife looked up to see Jud Mahley and his two companions crowding in for a look at the table. Hashknife glanced at Sleepy and Sody. They had seen Jud. Sleepy flashed a glance at Hashknife, who turned back to his game. He was not worrying about Jud Mahley now.

"A lot of folks wondered why Bud Daley wouldn't tell where he was the night of the bank robbery," said Hashknife, as if talking to himself. "I can tell 'em. I know. I know where that rosette came from, and I know who planted it."

The crowd stirred nervously. They were hearing something. On the fringe of the crowd a man questioned another. He wanted to know if he had heard rightly. Still Lavelle did not bet.

"Take yore time," said Hashknife softly. "I'll entertain the crowd while yuh figure it out. Yuh know, it took me quite a while to figure out why Bud Daley was taken away from the sheriff."

Lavelle jerked up his head.

281

"What in hell do I care about Bud Daley?"

Lavelle's voice was almost a whine. Perspiration trickled into his eyes, but he did not try to wipe it away.

"Somebody wanted Bud killed," stated Hashknife. "And it wasn't because they wanted to avenge the death of the cashier either. Ain't yuh about ready to back up yore three tens, Lavelle?"

With a nervous jerk of his hand Lavelle tossed some chips into the pot.

"Gettin' jerky, eh?" Hashknife laughed. "Count 'em, Lavelle."

"Eight chips," whispered a bystander.

Hashknife slowly counted the pot and found that Lavelle had bet eight hundred dollars.

"You ain't got much faith, have yuh?"

Hashknife threw in eight chips and added a thousand-dollar bill from Sleepy's bill-fold.

"There's a thousand that says my sixes win, Lavelle."

Lavelle swallowed hard and stared at the pot. His nerves were rubbed raw and he wanted to get away. Hashknife was talking again.

"Those pickpockets at Black Wells were disappointed."

As he spoke he looked up at Jud Mahley. The Black Wells cowpuncher did not have a poker face, and Hashknife's statement brought a startled expression to his countenance. He shot a quick glance sidewise toward the door and looked into the face of Sleepy Stevens. Then Mr. Mahley turned his head and studied the wall, but his hands dropped along his hips.

"Folks who don't know might think it was funny that they would dope and rob a stranger," continued Hashknife. "They didn't know us – except from description. I don't wonder that they want Lavelle to pay damages."

Lavelle stared at Hashknife, his mouth half-open, as if he were badly in need of oxygen. He seemed to have trouble in keeping his hands on the table. He tipped a stack of chips, and they rattled loudly.

"Sounds like a skeleton," laughed Hashknife. "Didja ever hear a skeleton rattle, Lavelle?"

"Damn you!" breathed Lavelle. "What's all this talk about? What damages? I never –"

Breed shoved his way to the table, and behind him was Uncle Jimmy – a very angry Uncle Jimmy.

"They got Bud, Hashknife," he said. "The sheriff brought him in."

"Don't worry about it," soothed Hashknife.

283

"Don't you worry about anythin' either, Hashknife," laughed Sleepy. "Go ahead and play the game."

Lavelle shaded his eyes with his hand as he slowly counted out his chips. Then he shoved thirty chips to the centre of the table; a thousand dollars to call Hashknife's raise, and a two thousand dollar tilt to the pot.

He did not say a word, but leaned back, dropping his hands to his lap. Hashknife grinned widely as he said:

"You bet that money just like it was the last bet you'd ever make, Lavelle. I wonder if you had a hunch. Gamblers do have hunches, don't they? I've got one, too. But my hunch is backed up by good-luck. And yore good-luck is gone, Lavelle. Right now you think you've got me beat, but yo're all wrong. I got you in this game to prove that yore luck was gone, and –"

"Play cards, damn you!" snarled Lavelle. "I've got you beat, and you know it. Go ahead and call my bet – if you dare."

Hashknife leaned across the table, his face suddenly serious, his voice ominous.

"I'm goin' to call that bet, Lavelle. There's a black cat settin' on yore shoulder, look'n at yuh."

Lavelle twitched quickly, and his eyes flashed sidewise. Hashknife laughed, as

284

he shoved in two thousand dollars. Then something flashed in the lamplight as he tossed an object to the centre of the table, where it rattled among the chips.

"I'll raise yuh that much, Lavelle."

Lavelle jerked forward, staring at the object. It was the rosette that had been found on the vault floor. Breed gasped and shifted his feet. Lavelle licked his lips and stared at it.

The crowd around the table surged forward, anxious to see what Hashknife had thrown on the table. Under the lights the hammered silver rosette flashed brightly.

"What is it?" whispered a voice in the crowd.

"Don't shove, you darn fool! It's a rosette."

"The rosette Bud Daley lost when he robbed the bank!"

"Where did this feller get it?"

"It'll take everythin' yuh own to cover that, Lavelle," Hashknife's voice was low, but every one heard him. "That represents a lot of misery, murder and money. You had it once, Lavelle. You got it the night you was out at Bud's ranch – that night, Lavelle."

Lavelle did not speak. It is doubtful whether he could have spoken. His eyes met Hashknife's, and Hashknife was not smiling. He reached slowly into his vest pocket, clenched his hand and extended it across the table and almost under Lavelle's nose.

"It'll take everythin' yuh own to call that last raise, Lavelle," he said. "But yuh can't win. The god of luck deserted yuh the night that the train was held up; the night you took Bud Daley away from Dug Breed; the night you had the boys from the 76-A hold up the express car so that you could have a chance to take Bud away from the sheriff."

There was not a sound, except the heavy breathing of the crowd. Lavelle seemed to turn to stone under the accusation.

"You lost your luck that night, Lavelle. It's here in my hand. You had 'em dope and rob us at Black Wells, thinkin' I'd have it with me. You had Jud Mahley try to kill me, but he made a mistake and killed Charley Morse."

"All lies!" breathed Lavelle. His lips barely moved, but his eyes looked straight ahead. "You can't prove it – you can't."

"It proves itself," said Hashknife. "You stole Bud's cows to try and break him, Lavelle. Then you robbed the bank to send him to the penitentiary. You dirty coyote, you wanted Bud's wife. But she told you that she was Bud's wife as long

286

as he lived; so you took him away from the law, hoping that he would be killed before being taken. Here's what broke yuh, Lavelle."

Hashknife opened his hand. It was a piece of silver, about the size of a half-dollar. As swift as the slash of a cat, Lavelle struck Hashknife's hand aside and flung himself backward, drawing a gun from the side-pocket of his coat, while the crowd behind him scattered like a covey of frightened quail.

But if Lavelle acted quickly, Hashknife was prepared. His two hands flashed to the edge of the table, as he flung himself forward, throwing the weight of the over-turning table into Lavelle, who promptly went over backward, crashing to the floor with his chair under him and the edge of the heavy table across his throat. Lavelle's gun exploded, sending a bullet screeching along the floor and into the boot-heel of a cowboy, who jumped high from the impact.

The crash of Lavelle's gun blended with the roar of Sleepy's six-shooter. Jud Mahley's right hand relaxed from around the butt of his cocked gun and his close-set eyes blinked foolishly as he tried to reason out why certain things were being done. For instance, why were several men struggling, cursing, fighting beside him; why were men shouting? Then the earth was jerked from under Jud Mahley.

Hashknife rolled the table-edge off Lavelle's throat and kicked the revolver out of his nerveless hand. Mahley's two companions were down on the floor, with Sody and Sleepy astride them, while Dug Breed jerked this way and that way, trying to figure out what to do first.

"Well, you danged jumpin'-jack, get us some ropes," yelled Sleepy. "Do yuh think we want to set on 'em until they petrify."

Breed turned to obey the order, but men were already producing ropes to tie up Lavelle and the two men from Black Wells. Jud Mahley needed no rope. Monte Sells and Brent Allard had disappeared in the confusion, picking up Frank Asher and Mesa Caldwell at the 76-A and leaving only the tracks of four horses to show that they were all through with the Modoc country.

Hashknife gathered up his money from the floor and walked outside, while men tugged at his sleeve and demanded that he tell them the whole story. Uncle Jimmy shoved them aside and grabbed Hashknife with both hands.

"One of them punchers confessed to stealin' cows!" he blurted. "Lavelle hired 'em to do it.

And Lavelle gave Mahley the shotgun to kill yuh with. You sure was right, Hashknife. I've got to tell Ma and May."

He ran across the street toward the sheriff's office, and Hashknife followed him. The crowd had already got there with Lavelle and the two punchers. Bud was lying on the sheriff's cot, exhausted from the rough ride, but conscious.

The crowd almost mobbed Bud, trying to exhibit their glee in his exoneration; but he did not know what it was all about. His wife, white of face, her eyes staring with fright, watched them and listened with ears that caught only a jumble of words.

Then Cleve Lavelle and the two cowboys were pushed roughly past her and into the cells at the rear, while Uncle Jimmy almost knocked her down in his joy and excitement.

"Bud is cleared!" he shouted in her face. "Don'tcha know what I'm sayin'? I tell yuh, he's cleared!"

She tried to smile. It was like a dream. He shook her violently, as if trying to force her to understand. Ma Miller caught him by the arm and yanked him away.

"Don't shake her, you ninny!" grunted Ma. "What happened, Jim? Tell me what happened?"

She shook him roughly with both hands.

"Don't shake me, woman!" he exploded. "I'm jist about to bust."

Hashknife came in and Uncle Jimmy pointed at him.

"He done it – the son of a gun – he done it! I tell yuh, he was the one what done it. I dunno how he done it, but he did."

Dinah Blewette shoved in and tried to shake hands with Mrs. Daley. For once in his life, Dinah did not try to talk.

"What is it all about?" queried Mrs. Daley. "I – I don't –"

"It means that Bud is cleared," explained Sody. "Lavelle was the guilty man. Hashknife Hartley put the deadwood on him."

Mrs. Daley lifted her head and looked at Hashknife, her eyes filling with tears of gratitude. Bud had lifted on one elbow and the men stepped aside to let him see what was going on. They had told him enough to let him know that he was cleared. Hashknife looked at Bud and a smile came to his face, as he said:

"Bud, I'm comin' back some day, when yo're well. And I'm goin' to knock hell out of yuh for believin' somethin' that yuh only heard one side of."

Bud blinked painfully and looked at his wife, who was coming toward him, her hands outstretched. He knew what Hashknife meant.

"All right, Hashknife," he said hoarsely. "I hope you'll come soon; and I'll take the lickin' with my hands down."

Hashknife turned and faced Breed, who gripped his hand tightly.

"Monte Sells and Brent Allard pulled out," he whispered.

"I know it," replied Hashknife. "But you don't need 'em. They were technically guilty, thasall. Mebbe they'll do better now."

"They'll have twelve hours' lead," said Breed meaningly. "Mebbe this will be a lesson to 'em. It ought to, anyway. I reckon we'll have to settle up Lavelle's estate and square things with Bud. He owes Lavelle five thousand, and Lavelle owes him for a lot of cows; but we'll see that Bud gets a square deal and that nobody suffers from it, Hartley."

Hashknife nodded and walked out, with Sleepy treading on his heels. Some one called their names, but they did not heed. Came the whistle of the southbound train, late as usual. They turned and headed for the depot, where they climbed aboard the creaking smoker and sat down.

A moment later the car lurched ahead, and the lights of Modoc passed from view.

Sleepy's nose squeaked on the window glass as Hashknife said:

"Gimme yore Durham, Sleepy."

"Why don'tcha buy yuh some once in a while?"

He handed over the sack and leaned back against the seat.

"Where did yuh get that rosette, Hashknife?" he asked.

"From Breed. I took one of the plain ones off my own chaps and had it in my pocket. When Breed showed me that rosette, I palmed it and put the other one in the drawer. I thought it would shock Mr. Lavelle. I had to bluff, Sleepy. I wasn't sure of it all, but I reckon I guessed right. Here's what was among that money that the hold-up man gave me that night."

Hashknife drew out the piece of silver. It was so badly worn that the engraving and inscription were hardly visible; showing that it had been carried and handled much. One side was blank. The other showed the faint outline of a shield, on which was a tiger springing to the attack.

It was surrounded with a ribbon bearing the faint inscription in Latin:

In hoc signo spes mea

And below was the one word – LAVELLE.

"What does it mean?" asked Sleepy. "I *sabe* the Lavelle, but I dunno that other jargon."

"It's Latin, Sleepy. I had quite a time with it m'self. It's been a long time since I studied Latin, but I managed to make it out. It means – In this sign is my hope. That shield and tiger must be the family crest of the Lavelle family.

"I knew that nobody but Lavelle would have it; so I had him dead to rights. He made a bad mistake that night. When they doped us at Black Wells, I knew they were tryin' to get it back for him. Yuh remember, I told him we were goin' there?

"I knew that Lavelle turned Bud loose that night, but it sure took me a long time to find out why. A streak of bad luck hit the Rest Ye All, and Lavelle got superstitious. I made a guess that he had told Monte Sells that the big pay-roll money was comin' through that night. He had to have that hold-up pulled off, and nobody but his own gang would do it. He had Jud Mahley with him that night, because Jud was the only one he could trust."

"And Lavelle was in love with May Daley," mused Sleepy. "That's funny, ain't it?"

"Funny?" Hashknife looked sideways at

Sleepy. "What in hell is so funny about that?"

Sleepy's mouth formed an unspoken "Oh!" and he settled down in the seat, while the car wheels sent out their *clickety-click, clickety-click,* and the engine whistled dismally around the sharp curves of the Modoc hills. Hashknife sat humped in his seat, his eyes half-shut in speculation.

"Whatcha thinkin' about, cowboy?" asked Sleepy.

"About a range where there ain't no more trouble, Sleepy. I'm kinda tired of it all now. I'm gettin' so that I can't think fast, and m' gun-hand kinda cramps on me – kinda. Ho, hum-m-m!"

Sleepy glanced sideways at him and grinned softly.

"Yore medicine is still good, Hashknife. When you git so danged old that yuh can't walk no longer, I'll put yuh in a wheel-chair, hang a sign around yore neck and take yuh along with me."

"A sign on my neck?" laughed Hashknife. "What do yuh mean?"

"Jist a sign," smiled Sleepy. "And on it I'll have printed: *'In hoc signo spes mea.'* Only I'll have yuh find me the Latin word for 'under' instead of 'in.' "

And the medicine-man smiled in appreciation.

294

The publishers hope that this book has given you enjoyable reading. Large Print Books are specially designed to be as easy to see and hold as possible. If you wish a complete list of our books, please ask at your local library or write directly to: Curley Publishing, Inc., P.O. Box 37, South Yarmouth, Massachusetts, 02664.